"Is this the problem?"

Diana looked puzzled and a little suspicious . . . and more expectant than she'd intended.

Drew supressed a grin. "Well, sort of."

On shaky legs, she circled the tub. "I can't see anything wrong with this bath. Other than the mystery of how it got here, of course, filled with water, complete with bubbles." She sniffed the air. "Magnolia?"

Drew shook his head. "Wild jasmine. It's guaranteed."

"To do what?"

"Whatever I want it t⊔ ⊔⊔⊔⊔ ⊔es laughed at her. "And wh⊔⊔⊔ ⊔⊔⊔⊔ ⊔⊔," he added, slow⊔⊔ ⊔⊔⊔⊔ ⊔⊔⊔⊔ ⊔se, "is to relax a⊔⊔ ⊔⊔⊔⊔ ⊔⊔⊔⊔ ⊔⊔. Milad⊔⊔

Almost ⊔⊔⊔⊔ ⊔⊔⊔⊔ did exactly as he instructe⊔⊔ ⊔⊔⊔ ⊔me she'd settled back among the ⊔⊔⊔⊔ant bubbles, Diana was convinced of the magical and erotic properties of wild jasmine. . . .

Shirley Larson wrote *Building on Dreams* because she "couldn't let Drew die." He's the virile cousin of the hero in *Laughter in the Rain*, one of Shirley's previous Temptations. The author also thought there had to be more to life for Diana, the sister in yet another Temptation. So Shirley brought her back to spar with Drew.

When she isn't pairing off characters for romance, Shirley enjoys married life—in the post child-raising phase—with her husband, Don, in Upstate New York. Shirley has also written under the pseudonym Shirley Hart.

Books by Shirley Larson

HARLEQUIN TEMPTATION
64–WHERE THE HEART IS
99–A FACE IN THE CROWD
145–LAUGHTER IN THE RAIN
178–WIT AND WISDOM

HARLEQUIN SUPERROMANCE
232–SEE ONLY ME

Building on Dreams

SHIRLEY LARSON

Harlequin Books

TORONTO • NEW YORK • LONDON
AMSTERDAM • PARIS • SYDNEY • HAMBURG
STOCKHOLM • ATHENS • TOKYO • MILAN

Published August 1988

ISBN 0-373-25314-1

Printed in U.S.A.

1

MONEY. TONS OF MONEY pouring like rain onto the South Dakota prairie.

Diana Powell envisioned herself drowning in money, wafting through the door of the bank. She would pluck a packet of one-hundred-dollar bills from the torrent, rip off the paper bands and scatter the twelve thousand dollars over Cramden's desk. A smile of faint condescension on her lips, she'd drift out with enough cash left in her purse to buy two new ten-ton trucks and a front-loader Cat....

"Double-entry bookkeeping is wasted on you. All you need is a debits column. Your finances are running a close second to the national debt." Jeanine, friend, heartless wielder of red ink and merciless voice of reason, stabbed a red fingernail at the account book, bursting Diana's fantasy bubble without a sign of remorse.

"I hate being number two. I'll have to try harder." Diana leaned back against the bench seat of the house trailer that was fast becoming a sauna on this unseasonably hot March morning and braced herself for another of Jeanine's pithy lectures on the creative shambles of her company, Powell Construction.

"We're out of money—Diana, are you listening? You owe six thousand on the Mack truck, five thousand on Old Yaller, your yard Cat—" she gestured toward the scruffy yard, where the secondhand Caterpillar tractor sat, its bucket flat on the ground "—and one thousand on what, for a better name, I'll call our happy home." A red-tipped finger pointed derisively toward the ceiling. "In addition to the big indebtednesses, there are little ones." She ticked them off on her fingers. "An unpaid bill at the lumber suppliers for four hundred dollars and eighty-three cents, that, like a bad cold, seems to linger on and on; a bill from Ed Watson for forty-nine dollars and twelve cents for diesel fuel. If I pay them, you'll be left with a grand total of—trumpet fanfare, please—one dollar and twenty-two cents."

Diana grinned. "Rockefeller, look out."

"Diana, I know you believe in happy-ever-after endings, but this is not funny."

"One dollar and twenty-two cents isn't much good for anything else. I might as well get a laugh out of it."

Jeanine tried to scowl. She only succeeded in looking like a lovely blond lady in distress. "Selling the trailer and Old Yaller won't give you enough money to pay what you own on them. Your only hope of getting out of this alive is to get a good price for the truck. If you found the right buyer—"

"I don't want a buyer. I want work."

Jeanine leaned back, and an eyebrow carefully darkened by pencil went up. "Then you'd better get out of the Midwest. Look, this was a noble effort. Working outdoors, being your own boss sounds wonderful. The problem is, when you go to bid for a job, you've got three strikes against you. One, you're a woman, two, you're a woman and three, you're a woman."

"Drew Lindstrom didn't sound surprised when I told him I wanted to bid on his project."

"Why should he be surprised? It took you four calls to get past his secretary. By then, everybody at Bernice Foods knew what you wanted."

"He agreed to see me."

Jeanine tossed a pencil onto the table in front of her. "I know you're the eternal optimist and you don't like to hear my pessimistic warnings. But just think for a minute. Sure he agreed to see you—why not? On the off chance that he *might* consider letting you bid on his precious project, you have to get in your car, drive a hundred and fifty miles and meet him at a rodeo he happens to be attending."

"That's the name of the game. I'm selling and he's buying."

Jeanine shot her a look that combined motherly wisdom and all the cynicism her thirty-year-old face could muster. "Are you sure about that? Maybe he's selling and you're buying. Why isn't he meeting you in that lovely thing called an office, where normal folk conduct their business?"

"You worry too much. He's been very businesslike over the phone."

"That just shows how smart he is. For all he knows, you could look like King Kong's cousin. But when he sees that dark hair, those blue eyes and legs that don't quit, he might decide to ask for a little something on the side, like that nerd did in Sioux Falls."

Diana flashed a smile. "And like the nerd in Sioux Falls, he'll wind up sitting in fresh cement."

"Won't be much fresh cement around a rodeo."

It was Diana's turn to look dryly wise. "But there will be something fresh I can push him into. Relax, Jeanine. I'm a big girl now. At the age of twenty-nine, I can take care of myself."

"I wonder. Remember what Rhett told Scarlett O'Hara about seeing eyes like hers over dueling pistols. If Lindstrom catches a hint of how desperate you are to get this job, he'll award you that contract . . . and go after all the perks he can get."

"He's probably married, or old and staid."

"Married, *and* old *and* staid doesn't mean a thing these days. My advice stands. Do you have enough money for lunch?"

Diana straightened away from the wall, feeling oddly buoyed by Jeanine's mixture of chiding and concern. She'd go after this job with every ounce of energy she had. If she didn't get it, it would be time then to worry about dissolving her assets to pay her debts. "No. I was hoping Lindstrom would spring for it."

"Diana. You can't go off without any money."

"I didn't say I didn't have money. I just said I'd let Lindstrom pay. Here's lookin' at you, kid." With a grin, Diana tossed Jeanine a wave and walked out the door.

DIANA KNEW IT WAS DANGEROUS to underestimate the power of anything—a storm, a job, a man. The grassy path led her toward the rodeo ring and, as she walked closer, she saw that she had underestimated Drew Lindstrom. Over the telephone the lazy South Dakota drawl had fallen into her ear as easily as sand slipping through an hourglass. As a bonus, he'd responded to her sense of humor. Despite her anxious determination to impress him, she was curious about the man behind the velvet voice. When he'd suggested the Clayton Rodeo, she'd agreed to the informal meeting without a qualm, thinking that he was at least giving her a fighting chance. His asking her to meet him here was exactly the kind of thing a man did when dealing with another man.

She *had* underestimated him. His blue denim jacket sported the word Lindstrom, so he was her man, but that tanned profile told her he wasn't going to be easy. He could be a thousand things, but easy wouldn't be one of them.

She sighed, thinking of how optimistic she'd been when she'd finished eating breakfast with Jeanine that morning and climbed into her car for the long drive. Now the afternoon sun warmed her shoulders, helped her ease out the travel kinks as she strode over the stubby grass toward him. The closer she got, the more the tension shifted from her shoulders to her stomach. Why hadn't he told her he'd be wearing a jacket with his name on it?

"How will I know you?" she'd asked.

"I'll be the one wearing blue jeans and a Stetson."

"At a rodeo? That's a big help."

"Maybe we'd better try it the other way around. Let me find you."

"Fine. I'll be wearing a pink ensemble."

Under Diana's boots, straw crackled. She thrust her hands into the pockets of her overlarge pink knit cardigan that swung easily over a matching vest and skirt. Some stubborn part of her made her continue to go to these meetings dressed like a woman. She *was* a woman, and she wasn't going to deny it by wearing jeans and boots when she wasn't working on a construction site.

As she neared the bleachers, a male voice murmured, "Those clothes aren't an ensemble, they're a brass band."

"What?" Too confused to take offense, she stopped
for a moment, puzzled, her head cocked. The man she'd
been striding toward hadn't moved, and he certainly
hadn't spoken. His attention was on the arena. Instinctively she turned to the bleacher seats on her right. Just
behind Lindstrom, a man sprawled on the second tier,
his expression amused. He lay stretched out as if pos-
ing for a centerfold, elbows propped on the seat above,
ankles crossed carelessly on the seat below. In between, his long legs had their own sweet way with blue
denim. A finger lifted to nudge the broad brim of his
Stetson a notch higher in greeting. "You are Ms Powell,
aren't you? Won't you sit down?" His voice was gentle,
his expression polite now. But those knowing green eyes
glinted for a moment, then went into hiding, like the
sun disappearing behind a cloud. "The man you were
headed for with such determined affability is my
cousin, Blake."

So much for Jeanine's warning about dueling-pistol
eyes. Drew Lindstrom had spotted hers at twenty paces.

At least her instincts hadn't failed her altogether. This
lazy, sense-destroying specimen matched his voice
perfectly. This was the man she'd expected to meet. Yet
that glimpse of his eyes warned her there was more to
him than either the cool face or the attractive drawl re-
vealed. A nerve skittered in the pit of her stomach. He
was ten times more dangerous than the first man she'd
spotted. This one was smart enough to hide his dia-
mond-bright eyes behind a friendly easiness calculated
to disarm.

Diana's long knit skirt wouldn't allow her to climb
to the level where he was. Trying to look calm, she settled herself on the first tier of seats. Just as she twisted
around, preparing to talk to him, he turned his atten-

tion back to the arena. She was left to scrutinize his hard profile and make an attempt at reorganizing her thoughts.

She shifted uneasily on the hard board seat. Rodeos were not her favorite form of spectator sport. With relief, she saw that the women's barrel-racing event was in progress.

The loudspeaker blared; a rider was announced. The woman's horse, a roan, pranced into the arena with a skittery pride. Diana knew next to nothing about horses, but this one had the look of a thoroughbred. For that matter, so did the woman. She was tall and graceful in the saddle, and the lovely flow of hair under her hat was the color of chestnut.

Drew's cousin Blake leaned forward, his arms on the fence, his entire focus on the rider backing her horse into position. Odd. Drew's body matched, echoed Blake's tension. Their faces took on an identical look of strained concentration, so much so that Diana could see the strong family resemblance she'd missed before because of their different coloring. Was it only a family resemblance she was seeing on these hard faces? Or was it the same emotion? Did these strong-jawed men both care for the same woman?

"Ladies and gentleman, let's have a big hand for the little lady from Rock Falls, Jamie Lindstrom."

Relaxing slightly, Diana smiled. Obviously, the woman was a relative. "Another cousin?"

Drew's gold-green eyes stayed riveted on the arena. "No. Blake's wife."

A chill little breeze whispered over Diana's cheek, and her perverse sense of humor made her think, *so that's the way the wind blows.* The thought had hardly cleared her mind when Jamie Lindstrom whirled her horse and urged her round the first barrel. The cousins watched with equal intentness, Blake leaning an inch closer to the fence, Drew sitting up.

A strange, inexplicable sting of disappointment surged through her. She'd expected better of the owner of that golden voice than an interest in his cousin's wife. How far did that interest go? Was it reciprocated? The strength of Blake's profile made her think it must not be. A man with the will indicated by that jaw would hardly tolerate a clandestine romance between his wife and his cousin.

She felt awkward suddenly, as if she'd eavesdropped on a conversation. She dipped her head, looked at her hands clasped over her clutch purse and felt uncomfortable, self-conscious.

Jamie finished her run, tossed a triumphant wave in the direction of her husband and guided her horse through the arena gate. There was a wait of a few seconds, and then the time was announced. According to the announcer, it was a good one, sixteen-four.

For an instant, Drew's face shone with pride. Then Blake Lindstrom turned, and Drew's countenance took on the lazy, half-interested look he'd had before Jamie had appeared in the arena. Disturbed, Diana forced herself to look away from Drew, and found she was the focus of Blake's eyes. Like Drew, he wore his pride visibly. Beyond Blake's shoulder, Drew watched her with sea-green eyes a shade lighter than Blake's. The Lindstrom men in tandem were too much for one woman to handle.

Blake's glance swung to Drew. "I'm going back to see Jamie."

"Remember your manners and say hello to Ms Powell before you go, Blake."

Drew said the words matter-of-factly enough, but there was something about his tone that raised Diana's hackles a little. Composing herself, she turned to greet Drew Lindstrom's cousin. He tipped his hat in a typical, gentlemanly Western way and murmured a hello. Under the wide brim, Diana caught a flash of green eyes, the flat plane of two smooth cheeks, one of them with a hairline scar.

She extended her hand. Blake Lindstrom took it in a warm clasp, his eyes friendly with a trace of shrewd assessment. "You're the contractor he said he was going to meet today?" A dark eyebrow lifted.

The hard, unfathomable man vanished. His concentration on his wife and hope for her success had made him look tense. Facing her now, Blake looked as if he were human, had a sense of humor. And at the moment, something was amusing him mightily. He cast a glance at Drew, the kind of analyzing look one man gives another in a poker game. She cleared her throat. "Yes, I hope to work with him, if at all possible."

"We're still in the negotiating stages. Ms Powell hasn't submitted a bid," Drew put in, as if to negate his cousin's implication that the decision had already had been made in her favor.

Blake looked over her shoulder at Drew, and the intrigued smile changed subtly. "I'm not sure I should wish you good luck. At a guess, I'd say my cousin isn't an easy man to please."

Diana's chin came up. "I've had a fair amount of experience dealing with difficult overseers."

"I hope so." Blake released her hand, touched his hat. "If you'll excuse me—" He executed a graceful circle around her and disappeared to the side and rear of the bleachers.

She turned to find Drew Lindstrom watching her with lazy speculation. The passion, the intensity she'd found in Blake was missing in Drew. Or was it? Perhaps it was there in exactly the same measure but more carefully concealed. The idea intrigued her. Suddenly, it was important to know for sure.

"You dropped your guard with Blake," Drew said. "Don't bother propping it up for me."

He was dangerous, more observant than any man she'd ever met. She considered playing dumb/innocent. One look at his face told her she'd never pull it off. With reckless abandon she opted for an honesty that matched his. "Was it that apparent?"

Approval flashed in those green depths. She'd made the right choice.

"That you were girding yourself for battle with him? Yes. But he charmed you out of your militant mood soon enough."

She opened her mouth to protest, then met his eyes. "Your cousin is a charming man."

"A trait we don't share, is that what you're implying?" One eyebrow lifted. She wanted to hit him. He had to know he was every bit as smooth as his cousin.

"Quite the contrary, Mr. Lindstrom."

"How gallant you are. I am about to match your sterling example of good manners." Before she could move, he whisked his hat off his head and plunked it on hers. He adjusted the brim with elaborate care, then sat back to inspect the effect. "Don't you know better than to come out on a hot afternoon without a hat?"

"I'm an Iowa girl. When it gets too hot, we find a shady tree."

"Not too many trees in South Dakota. That's why we wear hats."

Man-scented leather smell drifted from the hat to her nose. To make matters worse, the sun blazed down on Drew's head, giving his slightly mussed gold hair the sheen of a polished candlestick. The nerves in her stomach clenched in an odd, unwanted way.

"I can't take your hat. You need it as much as I do." She lifted her hand to take the hat off and give it back to him.

He caught her wrist in midair. "You didn't take it. I gave it to you. You already look as if you've had a touch of the sun."

His fingers were warm, lean, strong, alive. They enclosed her wrist easily. His eyes were just as warm and alive, glittering a green gold in the sun. His gold hair lifting in the breeze, he was nothing short of wonderful. He frowned slightly as if something displeased him. She forced her eyes away from his and for an oddly still moment, sat caught in the grip of his hand.

Sanity returned. She twisted her wrist, asking silently for release. He complied at once, yet his eyes held hers with tenacity.

After what seemed an eon, he smiled, as if she'd said something to amuse him. And as suddenly as it had come, the odd breathlessness eased its hold on her.

"You made good time. You must not have stopped for lunch."

Prosaic, she thought. *Yes. Let's keep things nice and prosaic.* "No, I didn't I—"

"I'll go get us both something. Hot dog all right, or are you a vegetarian?"

She flushed, thinking of how callously she'd spoken of eating at his expense before she'd met him, and how easy his offer was. "A hot dog sounds fine, but really you don't need to—"

"Can't have you expiring of hunger. Be back in a minute."

Common sense told her he wouldn't have given his hat to a prospective male contractor. Common sense told her he wouldn't have gone to fetch another man a snack. Common sense told her she shouldn't enjoy the sight of Drew Lindstrom in motion quite so much.

He collected himself easily and, with a fluid grace, lifted his body off the bleachers to walk the path in front of them to the concession stand. Inside the arena, another contestant ran her horse around the barrel racetrack, but Lindstrom never once glanced in the new contestant's direction. His interest in the rodeo had been confined to the run made by his cousin's wife. As Diana watched, hands were lifted to him in greeting from the crowd. He smiled and waved back. Evidently he was known and liked here. Equally as evident, he was a man who was attractive to women. Why was he enamored of his cousin's wife? Maybe it was her imagination. How silly it was to be feeling like this. She hardly knew him. His personal life was none of her concern.

It should have been easy to stop watching him. It wasn't. Especially when she saw his path was taking him straight to the area behind the gate where the barrel racers waited to see where they would place in the competition.

He went directly to the woman on the roan horse.

Diana strained her eyes, trying to find the now familiar profile of Blake Lindstrom in his hat. It wasn't there. The winner of the barrel-racing event was announced. Jamie. Even from a distance, Diana saw the woman's exuberant smile, the victory toss of the hat. The hands reaching up to snatch it were Drew's hands, the back it was hidden behind was Drew's back. When

Jamie reached down to retrieve her stolen property, his ransom was a kiss.

Diana forced her eyes away. What did it matter that he loved a married woman and she returned his affection? Diana was having a business meeting with him, not a date. The tightening of nerves that she was feeling was natural. The Drew/Blake/Jamie triangle had all the potential of a time bomb. She didn't want to be anywhere in the area when the explosive detonated.

The breeze tugged at Lindstrom's hat and nearly lifted it from Diana's head. Frantic, she grabbed for it and steadied it on her head. She wasn't likely to win any popularity contests with Lindstrom if she let his hat land in a pile of horse dung.

He returned to her with the easy stride that was becoming so familiar. He'd commandeered a tray from somewhere. On it were two foot-long hot dogs, their hot, juicy skins protruding from the buns, two packets of French-fried potatoes and two cans of diet soda.

"I didn't know if you wanted mustard, but I added it just in case."

"Yes, thanks, love it."

The cool breeze caressed her face again, this time laden with the smell of cooking hot dog and the tangy scent of mustard. The dog was delicious, the bun crispy with heat. She took a bite and then sat munching in companionable silence with Drew, while in front of her the hands were clearing the arena of barrels and preparing for the next event. The French fries were crunchy, the soda cooling on her throat.

"What's going to happen now?"

"Bull riding," Drew drawled.

Diana put her sandwich down, her appetite gone.

"Ever been to a rodeo before?" he asked.

"Once when I was ten my folks took me to one."

"Did you enjoy it?" The tone of her voice had alerted him somehow. He lowered his hot dog, and his eyes were on her face. She felt like a student being asked to answer a difficult question. "Not much," she said finally. "There was a young man who had hopes of being a rodeo clown. Inexperienced though he was, he climbed in the rodeo ring with a Brahman. The bull went for him. The boy was gored and knocked unconscious. He survived, but I never forgot what he looked like, being tossed up like a rag doll in those baggy pants, his red handkerchief flying in the air."

"Some people enjoy seeing others exposed to danger. That's half the thrill of the rodeo."

"Being exposed to danger and actually being attacked by an animal are two different things, Mr. Lindstrom."

"Animals are unpredictable, particularly wild animals like the Brahman. That's what gives the rodeo its excitement."

"Just what is it you're trying to say?"

In the dry, heated afternoon, with the baying and smell of animals around them, he simply sat and looked at her. "There's an element of danger in construction, too. You're a bit fainthearted to be in the business you're in."

Color flared in her cheeks as she set the hot dog with its paper boat down on the step next to her. She was angry, not so much because he was acting like quite a few of the other men she'd dealt with, but because for some reason she didn't understand, she'd expected better of him. "I've wasted my time . . . and yours." She gathered her purse and half rose.

With a quick action she hardly saw, he caught her wrist. "Add thin-skinned and impulsive to that list."

"I didn't know this was an aptitude test. Answer the questions and see if you're suited for the job." She stood looking down at him. "I'd like you to let go of me."

An expression she couldn't identify crossed his face. He looked surprised, as if he hadn't known he held her, or was displeased to find that he did; she wasn't sure which. He released her, his fingers sliding smoothly away from her flesh, giving her a sensation of warmth and power even as they left her. His eyes met hers, crystal green, clear as a Caribbean bay under the silky fringe of dark gold lash and brow. His shirt, open at the throat, showed a bare, bronzed hollow. "Very thin-skinned. It's obvious I have, in my clumsiness, treaded on sensitive ground. I'm sorry. It's just that you don't look like a construction boss."

Her chin came up. Stereotypes. Was the whole darn world up to its neck in stereotypes? "What does a construction boss usually look like?"

"Well, for one thing—" if his eyes hadn't already warned he was going to get personal, the lazy drawl would have "—they usually have hairier legs."

Drew waited for her smile, was pleased when she didn't hold it back. He could only see about three inches of Ms Powell's legs between her long skirt and her boots, but the curve of knee and thigh molded by pink cotton knit made him think the view would be worth waiting for. She was a lethal combination, this lady with her stubborn honesty, her feminine body and her vulnerability. Of all her traits, it was her vulnerability that bothered him the most. She was too honest, too open. She didn't have the barriers, the protection she should have had. It was a miracle some unscrupulous male hadn't already swooped down on her. She was a prime candidate, working in a man's business yet looking so delectably like a woman. Yes, she very definitely looked like a woman. A soft, delectable, vulnerable woman. How had she escaped the scarring process for this long?

He'd thrown her with his humor; he could see that. He'd better move while he had her off balance. He rose, grasped her elbow and aimed her in the direction from which she'd come. "You seem to have lost your appetite for your hot dog. By way of apology, let me take you to dinner somewhere away from the scene of your traumatic childhood memories."

"But I—"

"We'll discuss it at your car."

He cupped her elbow easily and pushed her ahead of him, making it impossible for her to do anything but go along. Beside her, he strode over the rough ground in his boots with elemental grace.

Diana chided herself for not treating this like the heaven-sent opportunity it was. She needed work— Lindstrom had the authority to give it to her. If he fancied himself interested in her, what was the harm? She could go along until he awarded her the contract and then—Even as the thought entered her mind, she came to a halt. "I don't think going out to dinner with you would be a good idea."

"Why not?" His cool green eyes took on a frosty cast that, rather than freezing her, burned. Those two quietly lethal words and the look on his face told her exactly what he thought of her insinuation. Seeing that look made her feel foolish. He said, "Don't you believe in mixing business with pleasure?"

"That depends on what business and pleasure you had in mind."

There was color in her cheeks and at her throat. She wasn't acting; she was disturbed. Drew felt a stab of contrition. He'd thought it would be amusing to take her to dinner. In the years since he'd left Rock Falls, he hadn't met a woman who intrigued him quite as much as this one did. That afternoon, watching her cross the straw-littered grass, her gaze fixed determinedly on Blake, something had stirred inside him.

Interest. She interested him.

He hadn't been interested in a woman since Jamie. Oh, he'd taken them out, fed them, flattered them, listened to them talk, kissed them. Occasionally in the past, he'd taken one to bed. Less and less these days. After the second encounter, or perhaps the third, he drifted away, leaving them with puzzled eyes and the kind of avid curiosity he'd grown to avoid like the plague. Quite a few of them had wanted to pick and poke and pry and discover his secrets and were far too willing to reveal their own. Women like that bored him. None of them seemed to have the passionate depth of caring that Jamie had, the dedication, the honor, the honesty.

But Jamie had given her dedication, honor and honesty to Blake. For Drew, that put her off limits to him forever. He and Blake had achieved an uneasy truce, and that was important, but his own self-respect and pride were more important. A man didn't poach on another man's preserve, no matter who the man was. A man retained his integrity or he wasn't a man.

They reached her car, and she studied him with the same wariness she had a moment ago.

"Thank you for the loan of your hat," she said, raising slender arms to slide the Stetson off her head and hand it to him.

He didn't want her looking at him like that, as if he'd gone to a school for male chauvinism and graduated summa cum laude. He took his time putting the hat on. When he'd adjusted it to his satisfaction, he said, "I had in mind the business of discussing the project and the pleasure of eating dinner with you."

Could she trust him? Obviously she could. He wasn't interested in her. His interest lay elsewhere. "All right."

"Know where the Coffee Cup Café is?" She nodded, and he said, "I'll meet you there at six."

THERE WERE A HUNDRED RESTAURANTS like the Coffee Cup Café in the Midwest, and at times, Diana had felt as if she'd eaten in every one of them. Brown imitation-leather booths, green tables, tiled floor, a friendly, overweight proprietress. Not the Ritz, certainly, but well patronized for miles around, known especially for its chicken-fried steak and lemon pie. The main dining room was filled with cowboys who had ridden in the rodeo that afternoon. Amid the backslapping and friendly teasing, Diana slid into one side of the booth, Drew the other. When the waitress came, Diana ordered a cold turkey sandwich, wondering if her order was more appropriate than she knew. That was probably the sum total of what she would get out of this trip—cold turkey. Drew protested her modest request, but Diana shook her head when he invited her to change her order. She'd be lucky if she could eat that much. Those bites of her afternoon hot dog seemed lodged in her throat.

Drew Lindstrom didn't fit in here. He was dressed the same way everyone else was dressed, in jeans and a plaid shirt open at the collar, and his hair was the correct length, but his elegant grace, his negligent posture set him apart. He looked like a celebrity trying to go underground and failing.

Strange, Drew thought. Diana Powell looked as out of place here as she had at the rodeo. She was fragile, delicate almost, a bright spot of color in the drab surroundings, a woman so unconsciously feminine that just looking at her made a man's pulse beat heavily in his veins.

She'd said little other than hello when they'd met at the restaurant. She didn't have a fund of small talk. That didn't bother him. Conversational lulls didn't make him uneasy. He rather liked the opportunity to study her without having to think of words to thrust between them. Evidently she wasn't bothered by silence, either. Or was she? Were her cheeks a darker shade of rose than they had been in the afternoon sun? He leaned back, bracing himself. He couldn't remember when he'd ever looked forward to a discussion with a prospective contractor.

When they'd finished eating, he said, "Shadow Gap is not a mining town, as such. It grew up as a resort around a natural warm spring and was used as a recreational area. We are interested in renovating the saloon-hotel, the bank, the school, the Fargo building and a house. Each building is in a different state of decay and would require different handling. We want the outdoor part of the project completed by the end of September and the indoor renovation by December 1. There would be a stiff penalty for every day the project drags beyond those dates."

Using all her control, Diana stopped herself from swallowing noisily. "You don't want much, do you?"

"We've already begun to create interest in the area through advertising. We're sponsoring a contest in which four couples will each be awarded a honeymoon suite for a February Valentine weekend. They'll be our exclusive guests before the hotel opens and be given the run of the town. They'll see our old-fashioned Western show with dancing girls, honky-tonk piano and shoot 'em up cowboys at the saloon, go bathing in the spring or spend lazy nights in front of the fire—whatever they wish."

He stopped speaking and looked at her as if he were expecting some reaction. She tried not to give it to him. "Does our time schedule sound too . . . demanding?"

"Downright impossible, I'd say."

He smiled. "Yes, I thought you might." He waited, letting the silence build.

She thought and thought hard. She'd expected to have to hire help and rent more equipment, but she hadn't expected a job of this scope and size. Even planning the logistics of working on several buildings at once would be a new experience for her. "What about access?"

"We've already contracted to have the road resurfaced. That should be done by the time bids are let. Tell me—" he leaned back and gazed at her, his face devoid of emotion "—how would you proceed?"

It wasn't a good idea, ever, to hedge, yet at the moment that seemed her only reasonable response. "I'd have to walk over the site first before I could answer that."

He nodded as if she'd given him the answer he'd expected. Outside the window, movement drew their attention to the sidewalk. Blake was there with Jamie, one arm slung over his woman's shoulder as he walked down the street at her side. Her eyes alive with laughter, she reached up and said something in his ear. He made a mock grimace; she said something else and he reached around in front of her waist and swung her off her feet and over his shoulder in a fireman's carry. Jamie cried out, "Blake, don't." He jounced her for a couple more steps and then let her slide down his body to stand in front of him. He wrapped her in his arms, and their kiss was hot, hungry. Diana looked away, only to have her eyes slam into Drew's. Like a flash of lightning, she saw the intensity, the passion. Instantly, the moment her eyes locked with his, he shut her out with cool indifference. Her heart pounded with reaction. She was filled with a dozen different things—regret, embarrassment and most of all, a sense of waste. What a waste it was for him to love a woman he could never have. Yet somehow, she felt better. For in that brief moment, when Drew had watched the woman he cared for being wrapped in the arms of his cousin and kissed thoroughly, Diana saw what she hadn't before. Drew's was a private war, one he kept secret and fought alone.

In a bland voice, Drew said, "My cousin and his wife seem to be celebrating her victory. They're entitled, it would seem. Shall we conclude our business by setting a date to meet at Shadow Gap?"

2

A CHILL OF PLEASURE SPIRALING up his spine, Drew slammed the car door and stepped onto the brick walk in front of the Shadow Gap Hotel. He felt curiously like a mother coming to reclaim a lost child: overjoyed and afraid to show it. His assistant Les climbed out of the other side of the car, video camera in hand, head lifted to frown at the clouds that floated periodically over the sun. A meadowlark warbled, and Drew's euphoria soared to a newer, headier height. He wasn't a believer in omens, but still . . .

The wind rattled a shutter on Banker Oliver's house, rustled through the trees. Drew had been almost afraid to come, afraid he might feel differently about the town than he had when he'd first fallen under its siren spell. He didn't. The seductive song still whispered through the canyon.

He'd chanced on Shadow Gap accidentally while on a trip through the Black Hills twenty months ago. He'd gone back to Boston and tried to forget the town. Instead an idea had formed, slowly, all the more tantalizing for its seeming impossibility. He'd finally given in. For two months, he had come home from a full day's work to sit up half the night at his drawing board, hatching the plan and honing it to a fine edge before he presented it to his boss, Courtney Hughes. He'd spent another six months battering down the resistance of his fellow executive officers. There had been more frustrating delays acquiring the property. At night he'd driven home to his apartment, telling himself he was crazy. He'd never been so tenacious about anything in his life. But he couldn't stop thinking about Shadow Gap. It was the first project that had captured his complete interest since he'd left Rock Falls and Jamie.

Now the struggling was over. His dream was coming to life.

With a shudder, Les peered through the video camera's monitor, then lifted his head. "This place gives me the shakes. You like this history stuff?"

Drew's gaze swept over the town. Images danced in his head of women in hoopskirted dresses and men in black suits walking the streets, their faces animated with warmth and life. "Looking at this place makes me believe, just for a moment, that I can understand other people's lives . . . and my own."

Les shook his head, the philosophy beyond him. All he saw was a raggle-taggle bunch of broken-down buildings. And Drew had to admit that under that bright blue Midwestern sky, his dream looked like a nightmare. The W. Oliver bank was constructed of yellow sandstone and looked solid enough, but the Fargo building next door showed bare patches of wood plank under the falling brick facade, making it look tipsy. W. Oliver's two-story house, frosted with Victorian gingerbread, had been built with gold-dust money, but the boarded windows were a mute testimony to the end of the dream. Behind the hotel the spring bubbled, warm enough to green the watercress in winter. An oasis in a shadowed canyon. A shadowed, ghostly canyon.

His town was an ugly orphan, but he loved it, anyway. Drew tugged his broad-brimmed hat a notch farther down his forehead. "Yeah, I like this place. It helps me remember I'm just one link in the chain of humanity."

Alarm flared in Les's eyes. Drew was amused. He couldn't resist nudging the young brain underneath that thatch of hair. Les averted his gaze, fussed with his camera. "Listen, this place is bad enough without you going on about links and chains."

"Sorry." Drew's mouth curved. His smile faded when Les swung the lens toward him. "What do you think you're doing?"

"Tall cowboy framed against a dead town; real fantasy stuff."

Drew had been away from teaching too long. He'd forgotten that the young have their own defenses. "Court isn't paying me to model." With a lazy hand, he reached out and pushed the revolving camera lens aside.

"I'm sure he'd throw in a little extra—"

"There isn't that much money in the world."

"Are you sure?"

It was a taunt. Drew didn't rise to the bait. He'd had too much experience with adolescent boys to let this twenty-two-year-old specimen fresh out of college throw him. "Yeah," he said softly, "I'm sure."

Les had the sense to look apologetic. "Maybe I'd better go shoot up some film so I can put your prospective contractors on separate cartridges."

"Maybe you'd better. While you're at it, do me a favor and remember there's a lot of debris lying around." Drew's eyes moved lazily over Les. "Watch your step."

Les was silent for a moment, receiving the double message. With the youthful humor he was capable of, he clicked his heels and saluted smartly. "Yes, sir."

Cool air wafted over Drew's face when he opened the hotel door and walked through the swinging doors into the saloon. His own image played back to him from the mottled mirror above the bar. Fantasy stuff, hell.

With proprietary ease, Drew edged up onto the bar stool, dusted off the smooth mahogany surface and settled himself. Ironically, the saloon had been the last to be abandoned and would be the easiest to make livable. It would do as a temporary office; the bar would work fine as a desk.

He stacked the blueprints in a crosshatched pile and reviewed his list of questions. He had appointments with two contractors, one after another. Diana Powell was his second appointment.

A frown creasing his brow, he drummed his fingers on the bar. Her contracting business consisted of a heavily indebted shoestring operation out of Iowa. Her one advantage was that she specialized in renovation. She'd redone half a dozen houses, two around Dubuque, the others around the town of Galena, Illinois, where Ulysses S. Grant had clerked in a leather store before the Civil War and there was much interest in historic preservation. He'd been able to reach three of the owners by phone. All of them said they'd been delighted with the job she'd done and pleased with the integrity of her renovations.

Still, he'd have to think twice before he handed his orphan over to her. She'd never done a job the size of Shadow Gap. Nor had she ever worked under such severe constraints.

He found it hard to visualize her in a hard hat, directing operations, barking out orders. He doubted if she barked. One smile would be all she'd need to get a man to do what she wanted him to do.

But this was a tough old town. It had had to be to survive for a hundred years. It was made of ancient wood and stone and rock that would fight back with a treacherous will. He remembered the way she'd been at the rodeo—delicate, vulnerable, unable to watch the bull riding. Was she tough enough to take on an old South Dakota renegade like Shadow Gap? Somehow, he doubted it.

He wanted to see people in Shadow Gap; he wanted to hear the sounds of music and laughter. He wanted that badly. But not badly enough to risk giving Diana Powell a project that would break her.

He wasn't eager to see her again. Of course not. He was simply... curious. Yes, that was it. He was curious to see how she would try to convince him of her skill as a contractor. With a woman's wiles, perhaps? At the rodeo, she'd been scrupulously careful to keep her exchanges with him businesslike. Now that he knew how much in debt she was and how badly she needed the contract, he wondered if she'd been as innocent as she seemed. He would have to watch Ms Powell very carefully. Not that that would be hard to do.

"Mr. Lindstrom?"

Drew twisted around. While he'd been thinking about Diana, the first contractor had walked in.

Tom Bridges had no previous experience in historic restoration, but his outfit was large, tooled up and ready to go. Yet the moment he stepped into the light ringing the bar, Drew felt his hackles rise. Bridges was big, topping Drew's six-foot-two by another two inches, with hands and feet the size of bear paws and a florid face that looked as if he enjoyed alcohol. Reminding himself that a man's demeanor had nothing to do with his ability to get a job done, Drew extended his hand.

When Les appeared at his elbow a few minutes later, Drew explained to Bridges that Courtney Hughes had asked that their walk through the site be videotaped. Bridges frowned and looked as if he wanted to protest, but then agreed.

After an hour's walk through the buildings, the three men returned to the saloon and sat on stools facing the mirror. In the cool darkness, away from the heat and the wind, Drew invited Bridges to have a can of beer and a sandwich. The big man agreed with such avidity that Drew found his dislike increasing. He fought to remain impartial. The South Dakota sun was hot; the man had driven a long way and was no doubt thirsty.

Conscious of Les sitting beside him and diving into his ham-and-cheese sandwich as if he hadn't seen food for a week, Drew deliberately launched into a discussion of the requirements he knew would be most difficult for contractors to accept.

"When you go over the blueprints, you'll see that we're interested in historical accuracy in so far as it's possible. We're leaving certain things up to the contractor's discretion; whether modern or antique brick will be used, for example. We prefer antique but we're aware of the problems involved in determining the quality of used brick. We'll expect you to contract your lumber supplies directly from a sawmill that is able to cut wood in the dimensions used in the pre-1900 boards that are on the Fargo building. We—"

Bridge's heavy eyebrows climbed skyward. "You can't be serious. Those boards are all going to be covered with brick, anyway."

Drew gave him a level look. "We feel you'll be saving yourself a great deal of trouble if you work with lumber that is compatible with what is there."

Bridges made no reply, but he seemed to be biting back the words.

"There are catalog suppliers of items like that Victorian trim on the Oliver house. We expect you to replace the broken pieces with wood that has the same integrity as the original. No plastic reproductions."

Drew stopped speaking. He'd taught school long enough to know a bored audience when he saw one.

Bridges looked up, startled at Drew's perception. Bridges appeared to consider hiding his uneasiness and then gave up the effort. Slowly the big man laid down his sandwich. "Mister, you're not fixing this place up for little-old-lady historians, you're doing it for tourists. Tourists who bring sticky-fingered kids and dogs and sand on their shoes. They come to these places and all they want to do is get an ice-cream cone and go to the bathroom, not necessarily in that order." He tried to smile but his lips moved clumsily, as if the movement was unfamiliar to his facial muscles.

"These points are not negotiable," Drew replied coolly. "We're looking for a contractor who will respect the historical integrity of this town."

Bridges opened his mouth, thought better of it and clamped it shut again. "When people start falling through rotten floorboards, you'll need more than 'historical integrity,' you'll need a damn good lawyer." He shook his head. "If I have to be hamstrung by this kind of bleeding-heart nonsense, I refuse to be liable to any lawsuits."

Level-eyed, Drew faced him. "We expect a contractor to stand behind his work and guarantee it safe for public use."

"We don't seem to agree on much of anything."

"No, we don't." A smile lifted Drew's lips, but there was little amusement in it. Thanks to this blockheaded man's stubbornness, he'd wasted two hours. And if Diana's business was as small as his research had shown him it was, he'd have wasted his entire day.

The front door of the saloon slammed shut. Both men turned.

"I'm sorry. I didn't mean to interrupt. I got an early start and—"

Was it the contrast of her yellow suit, her shining hair and her obvious femininity in the dark masculinity of the saloon that struck Drew? Or were his protective instincts called up by her obvious self-consciousness at having blundered into an interview with a competitor? He didn't know. He did know that by just standing there, she seemed to gather all the light in the room and fling it around her in a dazzling splash. He was staring, and he wasn't alone. The eyes of all three men were on her as she took another tentative step toward them.

She had the look of a woman determined to face a firing squad without flinching. Drew found himself wanting to reassure her. Infantile to feel protective toward her. She had defenses of her own. But to save his life he couldn't stop himself from saying, "It's quite all right. We're just finishing up."

Bridges, who a moment ago had been ready to jump and run, now scowled at being dismissed so summarily. "You consider our interview over?"

Drew turned cool green eyes back to him. "Don't you?"

"Not by a long shot." Bridges swiveled his big head toward Diana. "She your...friend?" He smiled, but the smile wasn't pleasant.

Even in the cool half-light of the saloon, Drew could see Diana's color come up. In that throaty voice with its husky appeal, Diana said, "I'm a contractor, just as you are, Mr.—"

She waited, but Bridges didn't supply his name, and neither did Drew. The clown wasn't worthy of an introduction.

"Not quite like me, little lady." He gave Diana a leering stare, then turned back to Drew with a wink. All he got from Drew was a stony-faced stare. His florid complexion went a shade redder. "You could've saved us both a lot of time by telling me this job was in the bag."

"The job is not in the bag. The contracts won't be awarded for two weeks."

"Hell." Drew could see Bridges was trying to laugh it off, trying to make a joke. "They've already been awarded. Not that I blame you. Can't say as I wouldn't do the same myself if I was in your shoes." His attempt at amused understanding was so patently false that Drew muttered a word under his breath.

"Your insinuations insult both Ms Powell and me." Drew's drawled words lay as heavy in the old saloon as the dust on the upright piano in the corner.

Bridges slid off the stool. "I'm wasting my time here."

"And mine and Ms Powell's," Drew said with cool precision.

"If this was a municipal project, I'd put in a complaint about you, Lindstrom. I'm gonna see your boss about this." He shuffled among the papers, withdrew his briefcase and stalked toward the door.

Diana's eyes sparkled with temper. "If this were a municipal project, Mr. Lindstrom would have a far better reason to lodge a complaint against you, sir."

Bridges lifted his bearlike head to stare at Diana. She held her breath and faced up to him, but her heart did a flip-flop. When he'd been standing up against that outsize bar, she hadn't realized he was so big.

Drew, watching, thought the lady had more courage than sense. The man had been ready to walk away, when she, like an idiot, had leaped into the fray again, this time at Drew's defense. He needed no defending. He was not sure the same could be said of her, for Bridges turned on her and said in a half snarl, "Lady, you're taking on a lot stepping into a man's world. One of these days you're going to get your comeuppance. I sure wish I could be there to see it." Drew stepped forward, ready to interpose his body between Diana and Bridges. Bridges shot a heated glance at Drew, turned on his heel and shouldered his way out of the saloon, letting the door slam behind him.

Diana started at the sound. She was angry at the man, and angrier at herself, knowing she'd made a mistake. Last night she'd been determined to show Drew Lindstrom what a levelheaded, responsible woman she was. And what had happened? She hadn't set foot on the site five seconds before she'd locked horns with a competitor. Very unbusinesslike. Could she repair the damage at all? "I'm sorry. I didn't mean to chase him away. Will he make trouble for you with your superior?"

"He'll probably make more trouble for himself. Courtney's handled more bullheaded men than you can balance on an I beam." Drew Lindstrom leaned back lazily against the bar, one elbow supporting him.

"Don't worry about your part in this. We were at the point of agreeing to disagree before you walked in. He only decided to put up a fuss when he saw his competitor was a woman."

Les let out a long whistle. "Too bad I didn't have the camera rolling." Then to Drew, "Aren't you going to introduce me?"

"Diana Powell, my assistant, Les Strong."

To Diana's ears, Drew's voice sounded dry, devoid of interest. Unlike his boss, Les's enthusiasm was almost palpable. He reached for her hand eagerly and shook it as if he were congratulating a champion. "You were ready to take him on, weren't you? A regular David and Goliath scene."

"I wasn't going to take him on." Diana gently but expertly pulled her hand from Les's grip. "I was just trying to make him see that I'm no different than he, no better or worse, just a person trying to keep the money coming in." She shook her head. "I don't understand why it's so difficult for men to comprehend that women have bills to pay just as they do."

"Some men have more trouble adjusting to the brave new world than others," said Drew. "It's lunchtime. Could I interest you in a pastrami sandwich before we venture into the wilds?"

She smiled. How easily he turned aside confrontation with that lazy drawl. He wasn't going to get away with it this time. "And have you adjusted to the brave new world, Mr. Lindstrom?" She climbed up on the bar stool next to him and accepted the wrapped sandwich he handed her. When he popped the tab on the diet cola and passed the can to her, she took it and drank, setting it down with a sigh of satisfaction.

He watched her, smiling. "I thought I had. Although I must admit I've never offered lunch to a prospective contractor who looks so good in a linen suit and nylon stockings."

She rubbed her mouth with the napkin he'd given her and met his eyes, hers alive with mischief. "Maybe you aren't acclimated to the brave new world, after all."

"If looking at you is all it takes, I'll adjust in a minute or two."

Even in the dusky coolness of the saloon, his gaze brought a warmth to her skin. *Easy, girl. He's indulging in a polite flirtation. Read any more into his words and you'll embarrass the man.*

She felt warm suddenly. Her fingers slid to the buttons of her jacket, flicked them out. The edges fell loose around her clingy silk tank top, exposing a long line of bare throat and silk-covered breasts. Instantly her eyes lifted to the bar mirror. Drew was looking—and enjoying what he saw.

"Make that a nanosecond or two," he murmured.

Stupid. Trying to stay cool and calm, she'd been provocative. She moved to catch the edges of her jacket together—and stopped.

His green eyes laughed at her. He knew. Worse, the rat was enjoying her dilemma. And the view. She felt a sting of responsive pleasure that was pure insanity. She'd come down with a bad case of it. She left her jacket open and lifted her sandwich to bite into it with great enthusiasm.

Yes, Drew thought; he'd been right about enjoying watching Ms Powell. And he'd been right about the fact that she needed watching. She was inviting him to the chase, but she was doing it so cleverly that he hardly cared. Never had he been given the green light with such skill, one step forward, two steps back. Never had he wanted to toss aside his lazy indifference and chase, two steps forward, no steps back. Deliberately Drew dragged his eyes away from her to meet her gaze in the mirror. "I have a question I'd like to ask you."

His timing was impeccable. Diana watched him in the mirror and put down her sandwich. He wouldn't say anything personal in front of Les. Would he?

Those green eyes dared her to wait and find out. Watching her, he said, "Do you eat anything at all between the times we get together?"

She didn't know whether to laugh or hit him. He'd led her neatly into the trap. With her mouth full, all she could do was shake her head. Had he led her on deliberately? She didn't know. If he had, he was a master. When she was able she said soberly, "Absolutely not. I know a good thing when I see it."

"Brave new world and feminism aside, you're not averse to taking a free meal when it's offered."

"You're not going to believe this, but I did think it was my turn to provide the food. I brought a picnic lunch."

"No."

At his mock disbelieving look, she said staunchly, "It's in the trunk of my car." Her eyes flickered to Les, who was watching with wide-eyed curiosity. "I didn't know we'd have company, but I'm sure there's enough for all of us."

"Good of you to be so farsighted. We'll have it later." Drew's drawl was lower, drier. "My boss wants a videotape of our walk over the site. That's why Les is here." Her eyes were lovely like that, wide, startled. Had she thought he'd brought Les along to keep from being alone with her? He didn't need twenty-two-year-old boys to provide him with protection from one small woman. "You have the right to refuse that request if you're uncomfortable with it."

She dipped her head in that way she had, and one long strand of dark hair fell forward over her cheek. "You sound as if you're reading me my rights."

Drew relaxed against the bar, one elbow propped on the glossy surface, his back to Les, his attention focused on Diana. "I just want you to understand that the taping isn't mandatory. My boss is trying this new technique to make him more omnipresent than he already is. And . . ." Drew hesitated, then decided to follow his instincts and be candid. "He's curious about you. He asked me to videotape the others, but he especially wants to see you. He'll be disappointed if you refuse."

She set down the soft drink she'd been sipping. "Will he take his disappointment out on you?"

Drew could feel Les shifting behind him, as if the younger man needed to release trapped energy. "That's not your concern, nor should it affect your decision."

Coolly Diana's eyes met his. "If this is something he's doing with all his prospective contractors, then I have no objection."

Was that a flicker of admiration in his eyes? She doubted it. She turned away, determined to concentrate on Shadow Gap and forget the man who hid his emotions behind a lazy drawl and an amused smile.

All it took for Diana to forget Les and his camera was to step back out into the main street of Shadow Gap. Renovating a town was so much more challenging than anything she'd done so far, so filled with dramatic potential that it was impossible to hide the gleam in her eyes and the smile on her lips. Elated at having progressed this close to the bidding, she ignored the scraggly weeds that caught at her nylons. In her sensible yellow flats she marched up the overgrown path to the school.

The nails had been removed from the door. Drew swung it open and waved her in, cautioning her to watch her step. Inside the cool, dank room, Diana felt she could sense the presence of wriggling children, hear the teacher, in the precise English she'd learned at the New York Academy for Young Ladies, admonishing them to attend to their lessons. Aware of Drew Lindstrom entering the quiet, dark room behind her, Diana stepped forward.

He tried not to like the way Diana's eyes roved around the room with rapturous awe, but he did. She was falling in love with the town just as he had. And as quickly.

"How is it possible that so much remains—the desk, the potbellied stove, the blackboard? Even the books." She touched the oak bookcase with reverent fingertips.

"When the town gave its last breath and died sometime during the depression, the children had long since been shifted to a larger consolidated school; no one wanted the out-of-date textbooks. The owner was something of a recluse. He roped off the property and was rather... aggressive in keeping intruders away."

"This is wonderful." She plucked a dusty book from the middle shelf. "Think of the teacher who taught from these books, and the children who struggled to learn. Perhaps one was the son or daughter of a miner's wife who wanted her child to have the education she'd been denied."

Behind Drew, Les shifted and the camera hummed. Drew thought of the picture he was getting—Diana

Powell, her face rapt with interest, her slim fingers a pale contrast to the dull brown binding of the book she held. He was glad he would have the film. And disturbed that he'd had such a thought. "Everything in here will have to be removed while the work is in progress and brought back again when it's finished." And he knew as he said it that he'd rather see Diana Powell overseeing that process than Tom Bridges.

He turned away. He was letting his business sense be led by his male hormones. He couldn't let that happen. She was easy to look at and easier to talk to, but he had to curb the attraction she held for him. As long as she was a prospective bidder, she was off limits. In the interest of fairness, he owed her that. But if she continued to echo his thoughts about Shadow Gap and look like heaven while she did it, he was going to be hard put to keep his hands off her.

A shaft of light sheened her black hair, spotlighted her straight back. Make that *impossible* to keep his hands off her. He was already wondering what it would feel like to smooth his hand down her spine and discover the pliancy of her body, the sleek curve of her buttocks. . . .

No, he couldn't touch her. He had to give her a chance. Getting a firm grip on himself, he turned away.

His answers to her questions became cool, impersonal. To Diana, Drew's abrupt mood change was puzzling. His conversation turned polite, his face smooth. It was as if she'd done or said something to offend him. What?

She scrambled to establish the rapport they'd had in the saloon, but she couldn't. He drawled the answers to her questions about square footage and matching woods as if he couldn't wait to end their interview. It was all in the blueprints, he told her. She did know how to read blueprints? After that barbed question, she stopped trying. She remembered her indebtedness, remembered Jeanine and the people in Iowa who were depending on her to provide them with work. In her desperation, she grasped at the one small hope she had of salvaging the situation and deliberately struck out away from Drew Lindstrom to walk toward the Fargo building. Exactly as she'd hoped, Les followed her.

The lady was too sensitive by far, thought Drew, as he watched her wander around the side of the Fargo building, the worshipful Les following with his camera. She had instantly sensed his change of mood and been hurt by it. It bothered him to see someone so unguarded. He muttered a curse under his breath and vowed to stop thinking such stupid thoughts about Diana Powell.

But when they walked together to the steps of the Oliver house, when he instinctively reached for her elbow to steady her on the tattered steps, he was more aware of her femininity than ever. To make matters worse, Les complained that filming inside the gloomy house without proper electric lighting was impossible—he wasn't even going to try. When Drew pushed open the creaking door, he was alone with Diana.

Belying Les's words, light lay in streamers on a faded Persian rug. The house smelled dusty, and a faint hint of must lingered on Diana's tongue. The floor creaked under her feet, the dry wood protesting her foreign weight after so many years of lying unused.

In one shadowed corner, a japanned table supported by four carved heads of writhing snakes that made up each leg. An upright piano missing several ivories had been placed against the opposite wall. A tattered fringed scarf of once-fine silk buried under years of dust spilled over the top. The velvet drapes with their frayed tassel tiebacks suggested gayer times, people gathered around the piano while a proper young lady played and another not so proper young lady flirted.

Drew watched her taking it all in. Les wouldn't have needed light if he'd kept his camera focused on her. In the gloom, her yellow suit was a reflector for the stray beams of light, as was the shiny darkness of her hair. Reminding himself that he'd chosen his course of action, he turned his back on her and went to the window to twitch aside a drape. Dust flew out, and he coughed.

His deliberate coolness made it hard for Diana to sustain her enthusiasm for the project. It appeared obvious that if Drew Lindstrom had anything to say about it, this would be her last visit to Shadow Gap. The thought brought a pang of pain. She wanted this project desperately. And not only because she needed the money. She'd come to love this place.

She'd never been one to concede defeat easily. "I'm going up to the second floor."

Drew turned slowly. In the half-light, he folded his arms and gazed at her. "If you feel a trip upstairs is necessary for you to put in a realistic bid, go ahead."

Her temper flaring, she took a step toward him. She was in the light, he in the shadow. "And that would be a waste of my time and yours, wouldn't it? Because you have no intention of awarding me this contract."

"No more than you do of bidding on it."

"I have every intention of bidding on it."

He stayed where he was, a dark, solid form of resistance. "With one truck, one bulldozer, one trailer and several thousand dollars' worth of debt?"

She'd been a fool to think he wouldn't bother to investigate her because she was based in another state. "If I get the contract, I can take out a loan to pay for the extra equipment and people I'll need."

"The logistics of tooling your company up for this job would confound a man with more experience than you."

"Now we've reached the heart of the matter. You'd be concerned about a man having to move quickly to organize. My being a woman makes you think I couldn't possibly have the skill to undertake a project like this."

"I have no problem with your being a woman. There are more practical matters to consider."

In his way, he was as closed minded as the baboon he'd made such a show of protecting her from an hour ago. Feeling furious and in some strange way betrayed, she advanced on him. "You're not being practical, you're being narrow-minded, prejudiced, unfair...and—" she searched for another, stronger epithet and found it "—male."

Drew didn't move. "I am that."

"You're all the rest, too."

His eyes narrowed. "And you are female... something other women might use to their advantage in this situation."

Driven beyond caution, she flashed back, "My being female is no advantage with you."

His face changed, and the change didn't bode well for her. He took a step, bringing him closer to her. "Why do you say that?"

He looked as if she'd insulted his masculinity. "I mean, I knew I didn't need to worry about your being attracted to me."

"Why didn't you need to worry?"

She stared at his face in a room that was growing darker with each minute. She'd meant to extricate herself; instead she'd made things worse. Much worse. His face was dark, intent and the look in his eye warned her nothing but the truth would do. Yet how could she stand there and tell him that she'd seen how enamored he was of his cousin's wife?

There was nothing to do but retreat from the field. She moved to brush past him and walk out the door. Like lightning, he reached out and grabbed her wrist. Her gaze flew to his face in shocked surprise. She'd thought his lazy disposition would make him incapable of quick movement.

"Why do you feel so safe with me?" The words were softer, but they had a knife-sharp edge.

She faced him, chin up. "You're . . . interested in someone else." The quiet rang ominously in her ears. He was close. Too close. She saw his mouth and eyes clearly. Too clearly.

"What makes you think that?"

"I saw you . . . at the rodeo."

Drew clamped down on his temper. "What did you see?"

If she told him the truth, she wouldn't have a prayer of being chosen as a bidder. If she didn't tell the truth, she would insult his pride. Either way, she lost. She lifted her chin a notch higher. "I saw how you looked at your cousin-in-law."

He went very still, but he didn't deny it. She wanted out of the house, away from the dark tension that sang in the room and burned in his eyes.

"I'd like you to let go of my arm."

She felt his body uncoiling, the warmth of his breath on her cheek.

"I'd like to show you how wrong your little theory is." His smile was a curious combination of control and mockery.

Excitement rose in her like a heated storm. Silent, the house waited. And now that he'd touched her again, she knew she'd been waiting, too.

"I can't—"

"Yes, you can." He settled her into his arms. "Give up the idea of putting in a bid on this project."

She expected seduction; she expected a kiss. She didn't expect a blatant attempt to remove her from the field of battle. More hurt than she had a right to be, she tried to pull away. Stopping her easily, Drew brought her arm up to loop around his neck, snuggling her elbow against his chest.

Shocked, caught in the friendly prelude to a lovers' embrace, Diana was too confused to offer him resistance. When he urged her other arm up to complete the circle around his neck, there she was, clinging to him. He'd begun the hug, but she was finishing it, and leaning against him, besides. His hands moved under her jacket, found and enclosed her waist, steadying her.

He shifted from attacker to protector with such lightning swiftness she felt dizzy. And confused. It was strange to be standing like this with him, eye to eye, hip to hip, the pose more intimate than a kiss. There was nowhere to look but straight into those green depths alive with . . . what? Sexual excitement? Amusement? Mockery?

The feel of his hard arms next to her ribs, the heat of his body, his hands on her were all strange, all new. All good. Too good. She felt a rush of elation. In this dark, dusty house, she stood on the brink of something new and scary.

"Are you worried about my being attracted to you now?" he asked.

That wonderful smile of his chased the fears away. "Yes."

"How worried are you?"

She tilted her head back to look at him. "Enough to scare you to death."

He laughed softly. "Let me take you out to dinner. Now, tonight." His hand moved up to play up and down her back, and he smiled.

Yes, she felt good. He liked the way her back was made. He'd known he would. He liked the way she looked, the way she moved, the way she thought. . . .

Diana tried to think, an impossible job. "On the theory that the way to a woman's heart is through her stomach?"

"You've already proven you're not immune."

"To your food or you?"

He looked down at her. "Yes."

She lowered her hands until her palms were flat against his chest. Warmed by the sun, the heated cotton hinted of more heat under her hands. Heat and strength. A strength she hadn't guessed was there beneath his lazy demeanor and careless smile. "Has it occurred to you you're taking unfair advantage?"

"You haven't got a chance of winning the contract. Why should I wait for two weeks to call you just to keep things on the up and up? Withdraw, and we'll save time."

"Are you always so impatient?"

"Never, to my knowledge." But he was now. He was more than impatient. He wanted to tease her, test her, taste her. Only then would the heat in him ease. Or explode.

"I think you'd better . . . let me go."

"Why?" He compromised by lifting one hand to toy with a strand of her hair.

"Because I can't think straight when you're so . . . close."

"You don't need to think straight. Just say yes."

His eyes hypnotized her. She wanted with all her heart to do as he asked. "I can't. There are people depending on me, people who are ready to work for me, people who need the money to pay off their farm debts. I can't let them down."

He released her slowly, his long-fingered hands making fire as they slid down her back. "I . . . see." He stepped back from her, depriving her of the warmth of his body. A chill shivered over her. His face became a cool, polite mask that hid his thoughts perfectly. "You did say you wanted to see the second floor?"

Upstairs, a corroded brass bed sat in the largest bedroom, stripped to the flat springs. She stood trying to study the water stains on the paper to see how badly the roof was leaking, but all she could see was Drew's cool face as he stood watching her.

How had she gotten into this impossible situation, anyway? Once, long ago, she'd thought her sister had asparagus for brains when it had come to a certain man. Now she could see just how easily it could happen. And if it wasn't enough that she'd met him in a business situation, she'd had to go and blurt out that business about his cousin's wife. What right did she have to judge him? None. None at all.

Diana grasped the brass bed; it felt strangely warm. She was wasting her time here. Drew Lindstrom would never award her the contract now. Nor would he ask her out again.

Full of trepidation, she descended the stairs. Drew was no longer in the house. She'd expected that, yet she was disappointed. Well, he was human, after all.

But as she walked back toward the hotel, she saw that his car was gone. That aroused her ire. He could at least have stayed to give her a few polite words of dismissal. Fuming, she headed for her car—only to see Drew step out of the hotel and head down the walk toward her.

His eyes swept over her face, noted her surprise. "Did you think I'd gone?"

"Yes."

He looked displeased. "Les had a previous engagement and he was anxious to get back to Hot Springs. I told him to take the car and I'd ride back with you." He stopped at the end of the walk. "If that's all right."

She was tempted to ask what he would do if it wasn't. "Of course," she said, matching his detachment, even though there was nothing she wanted to do less than spend another half hour in his company.

"I'm not ready to leave yet."

"Oh?" One of her brows arched in delicate mockery.

In the shadowy canyon, his eyes glinted with challenge. "You tell me you have good organizational skills. How about applying them to our supper?"

"There isn't much point in it now, is there? You've already told me I haven't got a chance of winning the contract."

It was his turn to look at her with gentle mockery and a lifted brow. "Is that the only reason you'd stay and eat with me? To influence my decision?" The accusation went straight home; he could see that.

"I hope you like chicken salad."

He smiled gently. "One of my favorites."

Diana swung away to dig her keys from her purse and open her car trunk.

They went back into the saloon and sat at the bar to eat the sandwiches and drink the wine. She wasn't hungry or thirsty; she was tense. In the flickering light of a candle, Drew's eyes avoided hers. She had never been a master of small talk, and he seemed disinclined to shoulder the responsibility of leading the conversation.

Drew finished eating and sat looking at his wineglass, as if the most important thing in the world for him to be doing at the moment was examining the shimmering paleness of the California Chablis.

She wished he would say something—anything. Her cheeks were warm, her body chilled. She wanted to leave but could find no graceful way of suggesting it.

He lifted the wineglass as if to toast her with it, then brought it to his mouth and drank. When he set the glass down, he met her startled gaze. "How are you at calculated risks?"

It took her a moment to register the words. "I'm not sure what you mean."

"My seeing you before the bids are let is a calculated risk. Both for you and for me."

She raised her head and gave him a straight, clear-eyed look. "I can't do anything that might mean my losing an opportunity to give jobs to people who need work," she said slowly.

"Perhaps it didn't seem so back there in the house, but I do respect you for that." He twirled the wineglass thoughtfully. "Suppose I give you my word that no matter what happens between us personally, I will do my level best to consider your bid with an—" he stopped, and his lips curved "—unprejudiced mind."

"That sounds fair."

"It is."

His arrogance made her want to smile. And his concession was so much more generous than she'd expected that her spirits rose like bubbles in the sea. He said, "In return, I ask that you consider my invitation to dinner with an equally... unprejudiced mind."

Her eyes flew to his face. She hadn't expected him to retender his invitation. "I'm never prejudiced about food, as you've noticed."

"Is that a yes?"

"It ... seems to be."

His smile was heady, heart stopping. "I give you fair warning. You may not find the meal worth the price."

She tilted her head and kept her smile pinned on her face, but inwardly she wondered if she'd been outmaneuvered again. "What price?"

"An afternoon spent in the company of my father."

3

"YOU TALKED IN YOUR SLEEP last night," said Jeanine to Diana. "You said 'money' seven times."

"I must have been doing an incantation."

"Your five-minute shower emptied the trailer's hot-water tank."

"I'm sorry. I was trying to wake up."

"You know, there is such a thing as giving up gracefully. You should try it sometime."

"How do you manage to climb out of bed before six o'clock on a Sunday morning with your guns already loaded? Even after that shower, I can't get my eyes to focus." Diana poured herself a cup of coffee from the tiny pot and slid onto the bench across the table from Jeanine.

Her friend peered at her. "You'd better get more than your eyes in focus if you're going to cross swords with Drew Lindstrom at this dewy hour. Why did you agree to go off with him at such an ungodly hour?"

It wasn't an ungodly hour. Early morning in the Black Hills was wonderful, actually—cold mountain air sparkling with pine resin, seasoned with bird song. Worth every bit of the effort it had taken for them to get here. It hadn't been easy. They'd shepherded their trailer and Sam, their ancient Chrysler, up the winding road to a private park last Thursday, Diana's eyes on the rearview mirror, Jeanine's on the heat gauge every step of the way. When the trailer was finally in place,

Sam had retaliated by settling in a rut and setting his radiator to boil.

"I don't know why I said I'd go with him." Diana sighed. "A slight touch of insanity, maybe."

"That's the first sensible thing you've said all morning. He's stringing you along, Diana."

"Even if he is, I have no choice but to take the bait."

Jeanine lifted her coffee cup, her eyes carefully directed to a point over Diana's shoulder. "You still haven't told me whether this is a business meeting or a date."

Diana's eyes flickered away. "Maybe a little of both." She hadn't told Jeanine all of what had happened at Shadow Gap with Drew Lindstrom. Jeanine had enough fuel to build a fire already. Diana had no intention of fanning the flames to a blaze. She tried a smile. "He said he had a family obligation to fulfill and he didn't want to go alone."

"And you, being the eternal optimist, told him you'd keep him company."

"After he promised to consider my bid without prejudice, I felt . . . obligated."

"A deft touch of Machiavelli. The guy is smooth. He knows he's only got a week left to move on you. After the contract is let, his number is up."

"Thanks for your high opinion of me." To the ceiling, Diana added in her Sammy Davis, Jr. voice, "And she's the best friend I have."

Jeanine shoved her coffee cup away from her. "It's because I *am* your best friend that I'm trying to make you see the truth. This situation is ripe for trouble. You're desperate; he's in a position to capitalize on that desperation."

"I'm not that desperate," she said dryly.

"Those aren't the signals I've been getting." Her eyes moved over Diana's face. "Go do what you gotta do. But don't say you weren't warned."

"That I will never say," breathed Diana.

AN HOUR LATER, amid warbling birds and pine fragrance, Drew opened the door of his gray Honda for Diana with cool courtesy and an unsatisfying smile that would have pleased Jeanine. But Drew's indifference didn't stop excitement from tightening Diana's throat. In brown cowboy boots, tan pleated pants and a cream-colored shirt, he looked edible. From his golden hair to his hand on her elbow, he was the epitome of well-groomed man with impeccable manners. Maddening man. He'd had long years of practice hiding his feelings behind that facade of easy affability, and he wasn't making any exception for her. She wanted to be an exception. She wanted to crawl under his skin and make him uncomfortable, just as he had done with her. She wanted to ruffle his hair and his poise. She wanted to see him driven to the edge of that superb control and beyond—Her mind skidded to a halt, even as Drew slammed the door, enclosing her in the car.

Six hours in this car, in his company. Insanity. Bracing herself, she settled in.

When Drew climbed in beside her, he spared her no more than a polite glance, even though she'd worn her red linen trousers, matching red heels and a sleeveless white silk blouse, cut so plainly it reeked fashion and bared one shoulder in whatever direction she leaned. He seemed determined to keep the atmosphere businesslike, so businesslike that Diana began to wonder if she'd dreamed that episode in the house when he'd held her in his arms. She smoothed her hands over her knees, wondering what to say or do. Really, the man was most annoying.

War had been declared, Drew could see that. She hadn't worn sensible jeans or a sensible shirt—no, of course not, not the uncompromising Ms Powell. How did she manage to look so enticing so early in the morning? Her smile was brilliant, her hair flawless, and the little devil was wearing a blouse that raised his body temperature several degrees. One shoulder was bare, inviting the touch of his hand. Or his mouth. He gripped the wheel more tightly. It was going to be an extraordinarily long trip across the South Dakota prairie if he didn't find something to distract him from the sight of that sleek, tanned skin stretched tautly over such nicely rounded bone.

When they'd driven out of the mountains and were skimming over I-90, heading into the eastern sun, he broke the silence, asking her polite questions. Was she too hot or too cold? She said no. She lied, because the correct answer was yes to both. Did she like music? Yes. He admitted to a dislike for the ubiquitous country music that seemed to dominate the air waves in South Dakota. Since he'd moved to Boston, he'd developed a taste for progressive jazz. Would she care to try Jean Luc Ponty, a jazz violinist? Yes, that was fine with her. His eyebrow lifted slightly as he popped in the cassette. Did he think she was trying too hard to be agreeable? She wasn't.

Diana told herself she'd accepted his invitation because he'd been fair with her and she felt an obligation to be just as fair with him, but it wasn't true. She wanted to spend time with him. What was he really like under the indifferent laziness that he donned or discarded at will?

He aroused her curiosity—among other things. Worse, she wanted to talk to him, share with him her excitement about the project. She'd discovered the most wonderful source of antique supplies in a new catalog she'd never seen before. She'd already lain awake most of the night putting figures on paper and making frantic calculations and seeing visions of a resurrected, refurbished and reborn Shadow Gap dancing in her head. Now she had a strange, silly need to share her plans with him.

Diana was just beginning to feel comfortable with silence and the sight of that full head of antique-gold hair lifting in the breeze from the sunroof when he said, "I should warn you about my father."

"Don't," she said quickly. "I had a warning once from a patrolman about my excessive speed and I didn't care for it at all."

He laughed, and she felt an inordinate stab of pleasure. Encouraged to further outrageousness, she said quickly, "Maybe you should have warned your father about me."

He flicked that sidelong smile at her that did strange things to her pulse. "What makes you think I didn't?"

"I suppose you told him you were bringing this smart-mouthed business acquaintance home to dinner with you."

Again the sidelong glance, the smile. She held her breath. He said, "Is that the role you're playing today?"

"I don't know." She turned in the seat to face him. "I've been wanting to ask you."

If he was stunned by her truthfulness, he didn't show it. Not a muscle moved in his face. "You're looking to me for direction?"

"It's your family we're going to see."

Watching the road, Drew seemed to be considering her words. "I see your role as that of an attractive woman I'm throwing at my lion of a father to save my own hide."

"Is that true?"

"Unfortunately, yes."

She found this revelation disconcerting but flashed him a bright, covering smile. In addition to the lovely Jamie, she had a lion of a father to stand up to? Dinner at the Lindstrom ranch was taking on all the appeal of a pie-throwing contest—with her as the target. "What a brave man you are, bearding the lion from behind a woman's skirt. What about your mother? Do you have a lioness of a mother, too?"

His face changed subtly. For one astounding moment, she thought she'd broken through his facade and he was going to be serious. Then he said in a tone that sounded determinedly light, "She was never a lioness."

"Was?"

"She died several years ago."

"I'm sorry." Inadequate, those two words. How long ago was several years? Had he been a young boy? She wished she could ask. His words had a bitter tang that aroused her curiosity yet warned her off. "Does your lion of a father have a name?"

"Thad."

"Will he be cooking our dinner . . . before he eats us, that is."

Drew smiled, the dry amusement back in his face. "Thad wouldn't be caught dead or alive in the kitchen. No, my aunt Ruth will be doing the culinary honors." He was quiet for a moment. "She's Blake's mother."

Ask—quickly, before you lose your nerve. "Will your cousin and his wife be there?"

"Yes." Drew drawled the word. And in that tone she was beginning to dislike a great deal, he added, "Actually, we're going to Blake's house. You'd already met my cousin and seemed to like him. I thought you'd fit in well."

Loaded with double meaning, the words hung in the air. Fit in well where? How? Drew hadn't admitted he was in love with his cousin's wife. He hadn't denied it, either. Had he decided to use Diana to buffer himself against his feelings for the lovely Jamie? Was her role to be nothing more than that of smoke screen?

The thought hurt. It shouldn't have, but it did. Diana turned her head to look out the window.

The car rolled across the plain that made up the middle part of South Dakota. They passed a herd of beef cattle, Herefords with rusty-red backs and white faces. Without thinking, she asked, "Has your family been affected by the low prices for beef?"

For a moment she thought her question was too personal and he wasn't going to answer her. Then he said, "No. My father is a shrewd business manager, and he's taught Blake to be the same. My cousin appears to have worked out a few refinements. Back in the 1970s, when everybody else was borrowing money, my uncle and cousin used their own capital from year to year and saved themselves the cost of interest. They made money then, and they still are. Not as much as in other years, but they're in no danger of bankruptcy. Then, too, Blake has the advantage of a working wife. Not that Jamie has to teach to swell the family coffers. She teaches because she wants to, actually—" he frowned

"—because she has to. She's one of that rare breed of people who enjoy teaching."

"I see," Diana murmured. And she did see more than he thought. She'd asked about the ranch and he'd brought the conversation around to Jamie, singing her praises. She dipped her head, wishing she were a million miles away.

The silence took on an alien quality, a quality of strain and tension it hadn't had before. Desperately Diana searched for a topic of conversation. "My sister teaches. Science."

Drew didn't immediately respond, and for a moment she thought he was going to leave her conversational gambit lying on the floor where it deserved to be. Then, in that drawl that told her everything and nothing, "Does she still live in Iowa?"

"No. She lives in New York City. Her husband is a comedian."

"I was a teacher, too. I taught sixth grade in the old hometown school of Rock Falls."

"Why did you quit? Burnout?"

"Something like that."

Diana looked away. How clipped and short his answer was. Had it been burnout that had led him to seek another occupation? Or had it been the need to escape daily exposure to Jamie?

After another small silence, he took the initiative, asking about her family. She told him that her father had died three years ago from a heart attack, that her mother had rented out their Iowa farm and moved into town and now seemed reasonably content staying active in the social life of the small town and spending her winters in Arizona. As the miles rolled under the wheels of Drew's car, they continued to talk. Their conversation was easy, yet Diana's nerves sang with tension. She felt wired, on edge, as if her body were filled with fight-or-flight adrenaline.

When Diana was certain they were going to drive forever, Drew guided the car under the signpost with two entwined L's, and they jounced along the lane that led to an imposing white, two-story house. A sweep of green lawn dropped away to yards enclosed with white rail fences. Clean, efficient, the ranch invited the eye. Thad and Blake obviously took pride in their land. It would be interesting to see them in action on their home ground. She wasn't totally unarmed. She'd had practice dealing with salty males. Her father had been well read and he had liked to talk. She missed those discussions. She hadn't crossed swords with an articulate man since Daniel Powell's death. A rousing debate with Thad Lindstrom might take her mind off his son.

When they pulled up in front of the house, the front door slapped open and a man came bounding down the front steps with no regard for his years. Diana took one look and knew she'd been overly optimistic—again—about her ability to spar with a Lindstrom man. Though his body was shorter and built more along the lines of a barrel than his son's, he was no less formidable. He came around to the driver's side of the car and growled through the door Drew had opened, "Where in tarnation have you been? Ruth delayed dinner an hour to accommodate you, and you're still a half-hour late."

"I'm sorry, father. We didn't make as good time on the road as I'd expected."

The bored drawl was back with a vengeance. In those few words, Diana heard years of passive resistance. Drew hadn't, as she'd thought, been joking about his father. The animosity shimmered between them like dust haze in sunlight.

"Well, where's your manners, boy? Who's that you've got in there with you?"

"If you stop thrashing around like a caged stallion in a stall, I'll make the introductions."

Diana held her breath at that blatant call to battle, but Thad accepted his son's provoking words with no more than a grunt and a glare. "Well? I'm waiting."

"Why don't you let us get out of the car? That way you can inspect the lady from head to toe."

Another grunt. Diana was beginning to see that this game of thrust and parry was a long-standing contest, more painful to the observer than it was to the participants. Her hand trembled when she put it on the handle of the door, but before she had a chance to push it open, Thad came around to her side of the car and acted the gentleman. She couldn't have been more surprised.

He slammed the door shut and trained his laser gaze on her. Instinctively she straightened to her full height. Eyeball to eyeball with Thad Lindstrom, she took the initiative and held out her hand. "Diana Powell. I'm a business acquaintance of your son's. I'm glad to meet you, Mr. Lindstrom."

His rough hand clasped hers, tendons and bones biting through his callused skin, his eyes no less sharp. A faded shade of turquoise, more blue than either his son's or his nephew's, his gaze devoured her. She hoped her mascara hadn't run or her eyeliner shifted. If it had, Thad would see it. His skin had that sun-toughened look of an older rancher, but Diana had the distinct feeling that if the lines of his face hadn't been blurred by the extra weight he carried, his cheek and jaw would display the same superbly molded planes as the younger Lindstrom men.

"Are you now? Business acquaintance, you say? Does that mean you're not interested in my son?"

Diana turned, searching frantically for eye contact with Drew, locking her gaze with his and wordlessly asking for assistance. He stood with his arms crossed on the car roof, smiling as if he enjoyed the sight of Thad's guns leveled at her. An unsympathetic eyebrow lifted as if to say, "You're a big girl now. Let's see what you can do."

Realizing she hadn't helped herself by inviting a second formidable Lindstrom male to line up in opposition, she straightened her spine. "Mr. Lindstrom, you have me at a disadvantage. If I say I'm not interested in your son, I insult him. If I say I *am* interested in your son, I embarrass him."

"Embarrass the hell out of him if that's what gets the truth said."

"The truth is we barely know each other. We just met a few days ago." Her chin came up. Darn it, these men weren't going to have it all their own way. She'd throw out a salvo or two and see how they liked it. "Perhaps you'd do better to ask your son if he's interested in me—"

Thad made a sound in his throat that cut her off in midstream. "I've been around this world long enough to know the male does the dancing and the female does the saying if she will or she won't. Do you find him interesting or don't you?" The heavy brows came together in a frown of pleasure. He was sure he had her.

Without missing a beat, she said, "I find *all* the Lindstrom men extremely interesting." She aimed a smile at

Thad packed with enough voltage to singe his eyebrows.

Drew laughed, the clear sound in the open air her re-
ward for persevering. Thad grunted, which she was
beginning to think was as much of a sign of his approval as Drew's laugh. As if her back-to-the-wall
courage had called up his protective instincts, albeit
belatedly, Drew came to her and slid his arm around her
waist. Under his breath, he said, "Beautifully done,
Diana. Round one is yours." The husky tone was
warmly approving. She felt as if he'd given her the
crown jewels. And to Thad, "Concede the field, father. She hasn't had her feet on Lindstrom ground five
minutes and she's already bested you. For that, she de-
serves to be taken inside and provided with enough
nourishment to fortify her for your next assault."

Thad scowled at his son and at the same time managed to look pleased. How did he do that?

When Drew's warm hand on her back propelled her
up the porch steps and the door opened to reveal a
young woman, Diana forgot Thad. Jamie Lindstrom
was even lovelier up close than from a distance. Diana
had expected to dislike her intensely, but it was Jamie
who, after introductions were made, extracted her from
the clutches of the men. Jamie took Diana's hand, led
her through a lovely great room done in mulberry and
blue, where an oval table was laid for a meal, and
pushed her through knotty-pine swinging doors.

"You'll be safe in here. Thad never sets foot in the
kitchen." She pushed a stool toward Diana, invited her
to sit down and thrust a glass in her hand. "I didn't
know what you drank, but here's a gin and tonic I put
together, thinking you'd need something tall and cool.
I remember only too well what it's like to stand up to

Thad Lindstrom for the first time. Ruth volunteered to oversee my stepdaughter Jenny's bath so I could offer you a haven and help you regroup." Jamie's eyes glinted with laughter. "I wanted to be out there to help you run the gauntlet, but I had strict orders from Thad to stay in the house." The breathless rush of words stopped, and Jamie's eyes played over Diana's face. To hide the confused emotions racing through her, Diana lifted the drink to her mouth.

Jamie shook her head with a rueful smile. "I'm sorry we're all falling on you like gangbusters, but it's just that we're so delighted that Drew has finally found someone he's interested in—"

Diana choked on her drink, shook her head, held up her hand. Grinning, Jamie offered her a paper napkin. "Sorry. Did I make that too strong?"

Striving for calm, Diana cleared her throat. "No, the drink is fine. It's just that . . . there's been a misunderstanding here. Drew and I are business acquaintances, nothing more."

Jamie balanced one hip against the island counter, a tall, frosty glass of cola in her hand, and frowned in puzzlement. "Business acquaintances?"

"We hardly know each other. I've seen him exactly three times—"

"And counted each one meticulously," Jamie said in a husky, attractive tone, her frown clearing, her mobile mouth lifting in a smile. "All right, have it your way—" she lifted the glass to Diana "—while you can. I see you as a reinforcement in the ranks and I'll go on hoping until I know I'm wrong."

The swinging door popped open. With eyes only for his wife, Blake Lindstrom strode across the room to her. When he would have pulled her into his arms, Diana heard her murmur, "Blake, please. We have company."

"Do we?" He nuzzled her ear, kissed her lightly on the lips. He stepped behind Jamie to face Diana and slid his arms around his wife's waist. Anchoring his chin on his wife's head, he said, "Hello, Ms Powell."

"Diana," she corrected him. "Hello, Mr. Lindstrom."

"Blake," he echoed her correction, and grinned. "You've met my wife."

"Yes. We were just—" the swinging door creaked again; this time it was Drew who walked through it "—talking," Diana finished lamely.

"Are you sure you don't mean commiserating?" Blake's hands moved lazily at his wife's waist.

A feather light touch on her own spine warned Diana that Drew had moved closer. She was still struggling with the shock of his fingers playing idly on her sensitive backbone when she felt his hand slide up and cup her bare shoulder.

Was Drew countering Blake's possessive stroking of Jamie? Irritated that he might be using her, she lifted her shoulder an inch to shrug his hand away. His grip tightened, making it impossible for her to break away from him without looking foolish in front of Blake and Jamie. Anger coiled within her.

Jamie relaxed in her husband's arms and rubbed her forehead against his jaw.

In a warm tone, Blake said to her, "Drew tells me you've already warned him he's going to be an uncle again."

"When Ruth called to ask him to come to dinner, she made the mistake of letting Jenny have the phone."

"I should have guessed our chatterbox daughter wouldn't be able to keep a secret. You were lucky she didn't know about the baby before you competed in that rodeo. If she'd told me, I wouldn't have let you out of this house."

"The doctor said as long as I was used to riding and in such good shape, there was no danger."

"So old Johanson said you were in good shape? Well, at least we know we can trust his eyesight." Blake gazed fondly at his wife.

Obviously the coming baby had enhanced the closeness between Jamie and Blake, Diana thought. Understanding sizzled through her with lightning clarity. Drew had snatched up the first available woman he'd come across to help him hide his affection for the woman who was soon to bear his cousin a child.

"It seems congratulations are in order," she said, flashing a smile at Jamie.

"So they are." That was Drew's voice, sounding normal. Still gripping Diana's shoulder, he raised his other hand, holding a glass, lazily in Blake's direction. "I salute your bravery, cousin. Has it occurred to you that if this baby is a girl, you're going to be the lone male in a household of four females?"

"I hadn't thought of that." Blake looked faintly disconcerted.

Jamie went up on tiptoe and gave her husband a grazing kiss. "You should be so lucky. If you twist the newest one around your little finger the way you have the other three, you won't have a thing to worry about."

"I'm a master of illusion," Blake murmured. "All my three women have to do is speak, and I jump. After all, it's a woman's world."

"He lies beautifully, don't you think," Jamie said calmly, looking at Diana while she nestled in her husband's arms with the complacency of a woman who knows she's dealing with a man who loves her. "If we go on standing here listening to his cunning propaganda, the dinner will be burned to a crisp."

The swinging door opened again. A sprightly girl of some age under twelve bounced through. "I'm supposed to come out here and see if there's any kissing or that kind of stuff going on, or if it's safe for Grandma to come into the kitchen."

Jamie reached out and smoothed back a strand of the girl's black hair. "Tell Grandma it's safe." Jamie risked a quick look in Diana and Drew's direction. "Isn't it?"

"Quite safe," Drew murmured from beside her. Jamie smiled and introduced her stepdaughter to Diana. Her resemblance to Blake was obvious in the color of her hair and the cut of her chin, but the child had huge brown eyes rather than the green of the Lindstrom cousins.

A slim, classically beautiful woman whose resemblance to Blake was unmistakable came through the pine door. "Excuse me. I must put the dinner on the table."

"Ruth, yes. I'll help you, but first you must meet Diana." Jamie extricated herself from Blake's arms.

Ruth turned, took her measure of Diana. "It's so nice you could come. We've all been looking forward to meeting you. I'm sure you must be starving. Everything's ready. All I have to do is put it on the table. Blake, either put on a hot mitten and help carry out some dishes or go pacify your uncle. He's pacing like a wounded tiger just because we're a few minutes late with the meal. Drew, see to Diana's drink, if it needs freshening? You'll know how she likes it. Jenny, you light the candles."

Blake flashed a smile, caught the crisp organdy bow at his mother's back and pulled the tie loose. "You're slipping, mother. You've just let Diana see who's the real boss around here."

Ruth tossed a mock-annoyed look over her shoulder at her son and grabbed at the apron sliding away from her hips. "Never mind who's the boss, just do as I say."

Diana smiled. "I'll remember that line," she murmured.

Ruth turned, her eyes sparkling. "You just do that. You might need it sometime."

"Stop." Drew thrust his drink in the line of vision between the two women. His eyes moving lazily over Diana in a way that brought up a deep warmth inside her, he said, "She doesn't need any more weapons, Ruth. She has enough of her own."

Blake shook his head in mock soberness. "You of all men should have known better than to bring fresh troops into the fray. Now we're outnumbered."

"I couldn't help it. I was blackmailed."

Her cheeks flushing, Diana turned to him. "That's not true. It was you who blackmailed me."

"Don't believe it, cousin," said Drew, his eyes on Diana, their green depths alive with devilment.

"Wouldn't think of it," Blake responded with mock solemnity.

Diana found the rapport between the cousins heart-warming. She didn't understand how Blake could be blind to his cousin's affection for his wife, but obviously he was. Or, and this was a startling thought, perhaps Blake did see it ... but he was secure enough in Jamie's love not to care. If those few minutes in the kitchen were any indication, that seemed to Diana a better reading of the situation.

As deftly as he did all things, Drew released her to take his place as a waiter in the line behind Jamie. He accepted a covered dish from Ruth, and with a lift of an eyebrow, indicated Diana should follow him into the other room. Feeling a flicker of defiance, she hesitated. He shrugged and turned his back on her. The moment he did that, she was annoyed. What right did he have to treat her so casually? She followed after him, determined to have a talk with him—the talk it was obvious they should have had in the car.

It was too late. Before Diana could get close enough to Drew to speak privately, Ruth's efficient organization had the food on the table and her family seated, Diana and Blake on one side of the table, Drew and Jamie on the other, Thad and herself at each end.

Before the potatoes were passed, Thad launched to the attack. "Well, my boy," he said to Blake, his tone oozing warmth, "I hear congratulations are in order." He beamed with pleasure, his gaze swinging to Jamie. "Long past time, too, I might add."

"We're glad you're pleased," was all Jamie said.

Thad turned to Drew, and in a rasping tone that raised Diana's hackles, added, "That give you any clue to how it's done?"

"Thad, help yourself to the corn. Diana, don't be bashful. We're accustomed to seeing young women eat. Take more potatoes." Ruth poured oil on the troubled waters as if she'd had long practice at it.

When Thad shot the older woman one of those piercing looks, she ignored him and went on overseeing the circling of the food dishes around the table. To

Diana's amazement, a dark red flush stained Thad's cheekbones.

"I do have a clue as to 'how it's done, father,'" Drew drawled, his eyes meeting Diana's across the cucumber salad.

Without missing a beat, Thad turned on Diana. "Are you one of them newfangled career women?"

Caught with her salad on her fork, she stared at Thad, several answers on the tip of her tongue. She thought of Ruth and said, "Yes."

"I suppose you don't believe in having a family."

"Quite the contrary. I'm all for women having children. It's an arrangement that's worked out pretty well in the past. I suppose the human race will go right on doing it that way."

With a serene smile on her face, Ruth said, "Put the hoop down, Thad."

"Why? She seemed to be jumping through it pretty well."

"She's a guest," Ruth said gently.

Thad looked like a child whose toy had been taken away, but the rest of the meal proceeded in a lighter atmosphere. The food was Midwestern delicious, tender roast beef, potatoes brimming with butter, crisp green salad. For dessert there was rhubarb-strawberry pie. Ruth accepted Diana's compliments with the same smile of pleasure that Diana had seen her own mother exhibit at the end of a successful meal.

In the afternoon they played a board game, Rummy Royal. Diana couldn't concentrate. They had spread the board on the coffee table in the living room, and while Diana sat decorously on the sofa, Drew sprawled on the floor beside her, his head against her thigh. He was deliberately giving his family the wrong impression about them, just as he had in the kitchen, but there was nothing she could do about it. Except feel the brush of his hair against her thigh every time either of them moved.

Drew had planned to leave around four, but it was five o'clock before Diana settled into the car beside him. Sated with good food, steeped in the well-being that several hours spent in pleasant company brought, Diana laid her head back on the seat.

"Are you tired?" Drew asked. "Go to sleep, if you like. I don't mind."

"No, I'll stay awake."

The car was warm, the music soothing. Her eyelids drooped.

SHE WOKE TO FRAGRANT DARKNESS, warm night air and pine-scented forest, the taste of resin on her tongue. She moved, and a light jacket dropped from where it had been thrown over her like a quilt. The car was parked at the campsite, under a tree.

Beside her, Drew lay unmoving, his head thrown back on the reclining car seat, his hand splayed over his thigh. She moved to wake him, then pulled her hand back. He looked too peaceful, sleeping there beside her, his face illuminated by the vapor lamp.

Diana prepared to slide from the car, moving quietly, not wanting to disturb him. A hand clasped her wrist, another slid behind her shoulders. With a strength and swiftness she hadn't guessed a sleepy man capable of, he pulled her over the console and onto his lap. "Drew—"

His hard thighs under her bottom, his arms nudged her into place against his chest. "Shh." He smoothed her hair as if she were a child. "You're tired, and so am I. Let's sleep together." As easily as if he'd done it many times before, his knuckles slid under her breast, the tips of his fingers warm and hard against her silk-swathed midriff. He settled his other hand on top of the first, locking her inside a cocoon of warmth. "You smell good; did you know? Like dew-fresh grass."

"Drew—"

"Shh. You'll break the spell."

"I can't—"

"Woman, you need a lesson in sleeping. First you close your eyes." A hand cupped her cheek; his face came forward, darkened the night. "Then you close your mouth."

How careful, that first brush of his lips. How much it left her wanting more. "Please—"

Another light brushing of the lips, slightly less economical than the first, slightly more maddening. Then another. And another. Her mouth was swelling in anticipation, her breasts lifting. Her body was learning to soar.

Drew went on schooling her in the shape and texture of his lips, lavishing on her his own special combination of sweetness and passion. He went so slowly that she couldn't protest each small slide toward intimacy, until he slipped his tongue inside and claimed what seemed to have been his right from the start.

It was joy; it was madness; it was . . . forgetfulness. Numbing, mindless forgetfulness.

Blindly she thrust against him. He fell back against the seat with a soft grunt. "What . . . is it?" he said at last.

She felt as if she couldn't breathe. "I won't be used."

Another long silence. "How am I using you?"

"You're in love with . . . someone else," she said in a low tone.

He made a sound of derision.

"Don't," she cried. "If nothing else, let's be honest with each other."

"Yes," he said, sitting back, not touching her but leaving her achingly aware of the intimacy of her curved bottom pressing against his thighs. "By all means. Let's see how you intend to play this: you pretend an interest in me so I'll award you the contract—something I refuse to use as incentive, by the way—but if I try to collect on all the lovely promises you've been flashing at me with those big, blue eyes, you accuse me of being in love with my cousin's wife. That's a nice, neat little scheme."

"You're wrong. There've been no promises—"

"Haven't there?" He sounded almost savage, very unDrewlike. He grasped her arms and lifted her off his lap. "You'd better get out."

Her head spinning, her mind in confusion, she reached for the door handle. And stopped. In a low voice, she said, "You're right. I have been... looking at you. You're very... pleasant to look at."

He sat there, still leaning back against the seat, his posture indolent, his hand lying elegantly along his thigh, his mouth curved in disbelief.

She gazed at him, her heart pounding. "You don't really know what you are, do you? You have no idea how... attractive you are."

"I know you have nothing to lose by saying so."

His cynicism was layers deep, but still the implication hurt that she was telling an expedient lie. "I'm telling you the truth, Drew."

He turned in the seat and, even in the dark, she could feel the glittering sharpness of those green eyes moving over her. "Well, here's a truth for you. When I touch you, it isn't my cousin's wife I'm thinking of."

HURTING IN PLACES she didn't know could hurt, Diana stood watching the red taillights of Drew's car disappear around a curve, leaving her standing alone in the whispering silence of the cool, resiny night. Hardly seduced, but certainly abandoned.

With the memory of Drew's warm mouth burning on hers, she headed for the trailer. Her arms were hot where he'd touched her, chilled where the night breeze caressed. Sympathetic crickets chirped in a sleepy, slow rhythm.

Inside the trailer, the night-light above the tiny table burned, not quite reaching the shadows where Jeanine slept tucked up in her bunk. Her one unconscious acknowledgment that Diana had come into the trailer was a sighing, deep breath. Envying her roommate's sweet oblivion and loath to disturb it, Diana undressed quietly, letting the silk blouse slither to the floor.

She'd put that blouse on with such high hopes that morning. Had she known the day would end like this, she would never have gone. She'd blithely let Drew Lindstrom lead her into the bosom of his family, only to discover he was using her.

"When I touch you, it isn't my cousin's wife I'm thinking of." Had he meant those words? No, of course he hadn't. He'd lied to her right from the beginning, telling her he didn't want her to place a bid because he *was* interested in her. She'd been fool enough to believe him. Until she'd seen him with his family.

Suppose by some miracle, she was awarded the bid. She would spend the rest of the year in close proximity to Drew Lindstrom. Could she bear that? Or should she just give up and go home? No, she couldn't do that. She had debts and obligations to people. She had to do her best to submit the most complete, cut-to-the-bone bid she had ever done—and let Drew Lindstrom deal with it.

If she didn't get the contract, at least she wouldn't see anymore of him. She'd leave South Dakota and look for a project in Iowa. Actually, it would be better for everybody concerned if that happened. It was what she wanted to happen.

Diana moaned and put her face into the pillow, trying to shut out the voice inside her head. *Liar,* it said softly. *Liar.*

IN HIS BOSTON OFFICE, Court told Drew, "Play that videotape again."

Drew hit the rewind button on the remote control. Stretching his long legs in front of him and adjusting the crease in his gray flannel trousers with an impatient tug, he concentrated on keeping his face expressionless through the second playing of the videotape on Court's forty-one inch screen. It brought Shadow Gap and Diana's larger-than-life image into the room.

The big man watched Drew from the vantage point of a relaxed sprawl, head laid back on his executive chair, legs crossed, heavy eyelids half-closed. Drew wasn't fooled by his boss's nearly somnolent pose. He'd seen Court put a man cozily at ease in the chair where Drew sat, disarm him with soothing talk and a silky smile and, with the famous heavy eyelids at half-mast, nail the hapless man to the wall.

On the screen, Diana moved, talked, breathed, and behind Drew's back, flashed a conspiratorial grin at Les. The little minx. Drew hadn't seen her clowning for the camera.

Inside the schoolhouse, the shadows couldn't hide her reaction to the dusty room. Her awe and enthusiasm were there, all recorded in the tiny dots of moving light that recreated her face and body. Her face glowed.

"She certainly does look . . . interested in doing the job."

"Yes," Drew drawled, "doesn't she?"

Now came the section where she'd walked away from Drew. Behind the Fargo building, she faced directly into the lens, her eyes dark, challenging, her chin up.

"There are twenty-one boards missing here, and—" she drew a small penknife out of her purse and held it up to the camera "—fifteen more that are rotten and will have to be replaced." She stabbed the knife into a board, and it crumbled. "There's a sawmill in Kinston that does custom cutting. I've already contacted them, and they've reassured me they can cut the one-by-sixteens I'll need to repair the wall." She was obviously using the camera to communicate with Courtney Hughes. His lips tilted in a half smile, Drew looked at Court.

"Savvy lady," Court said softly. "Using my camera to her advantage. I like that."

When Drew made no reply, Court stifled a smile and nudged aside a piece of paper from the sheaf that lay on his desk. "She's not only smart, she's good-looking. A formidable combination." Court paused, lifted his eyes to Drew. "Or hadn't you noticed."

A muscle moved in Drew's cheek. "I've noticed."

"It must have been hard to consider her bid with an unprejudiced mind." Court's hand stilled. "Yet obviously you did. You recommend awarding the contract to Porter Construction out of Sioux Falls." Courtney tapped the paper with an index finger. "Even though their bid is higher."

Drew looked at Courtney, his expression as bland as his boss's. "I've thought about it carefully. I can't in good conscience recommend Powell. She has neither the equipment nor the experience to—"

"She's certainly had experience in renovation. She's demonstrated that. You told me yourself Bridges wasn't even aware he'd have the problem of different-size boards."

A muscle moved in Drew's jaw. "Porter's a big outfit, tooled up and ready to go. They're South Dakota based and—"

"Their boss is a sixty-year-old man."

"He's competent—"

"And unimaginative. He'll do what he's told, no more no less." Courtney leaned forward. "I think this job requires something more."

Drew reached for control. "This job requires what any job requires, a construction outfit with the man power and the ability to see it through."

"You think Ms Powell can't handle it?"

"Not with only her present employees and equipment."

Courtney shook his head. "Won't matter. She states she has the man power on tap, waiting for a word from her." He steepled his fingers in front of him, his eyes on the TV screen. "I sense something of the zealot in Ms Powell. She looks like the type of lady who would work her buns off...." He paused, his eyes still on the screen.

Les had caught a shot of Diana from the back as she walked with Drew toward the Oliver house. Under the yellow linen, her hips swung with a feminine grace. Courtney smiled that half smile of his and sketched a lifted eyebrow at Drew. "Make that work her very attractive buns off, to get the job done right."

"I've never known you to award a contract to the prettiest face before."

"It wasn't her face we were talking about," Courtney said, his eyes on Drew. "Be that as it may; have you thought of this project from every angle? Awarding the contract to a woman will result in excellent publicity for our company."

"You sound as if you've already made your decision against my recommendation."

"I have," Court said softly, watching him.

Drew's temper threatened to take control. He reigned it in sharply. "Having her forfeit because she can't bring the job in on time would be publicity, too. Hardly the kind you'd want."

"I'm beginning to think there's something personal in your rejection of Ms Powell's bid."

Drew knew Court well enough to know that any display of emotion by him would reveal to Court how close to the truth he was.

"Why would I have anything personal against Ms Powell?"

"Why, indeed? This will have to go before the board, of course."

"Of course." Drew's voice was dry, cool. "But they'll do what you recommend."

"You think I'm making a mistake."

Drew had known Courtney too long to misunderstand him. Or to lie to him. "Yes."

"Well, then—" Court's eyes were nearly closed "—it will be up to you to see that I haven't." His mouth curved. He liked nothing better than to issue just that sort of challenge, Drew knew. Despite Court's apparent inattention, he was watching Drew closely.

"If she is awarded the bid, do you think you can keep Ms Powell in line?"

In that exceedingly dry tone that said nothing and everything, Drew replied, "I'll certainly try."

THE OLD SALOON IN SHADOW GAP was ablaze with light. His eyes narrowed, his mood dark, Drew lounged against a corner of the bar. From the beginning he'd argued against a party to announce the renovation of Shadow Gap and Diana Powell as the contractor. Court had prevailed. He'd lost.

The elements echoed Drew's mood. A gray sky poured rain on the South Dakota prairie all day. But despite the downpour, at six o'clock that evening guests bustled in the door, shaking umbrellas and shedding London Fog raincoats. Court attended to them with ease, handing their dripping coats to a staff member with one hand and guiding them toward the bar with the other. In minutes the most disgruntled, dripping lady was laughing good-naturedly at Court's apology for her ride through the "dry" Dakota prairie, and smiling up into Court's face, forgetting to fuss with her hair and looking suddenly very glad that she'd gone through all the trouble it had taken to arrive at his party.

The Bernice board members who'd been flown to South Dakota in Court's private jet, as well as the local politicos who'd braved the newly blacktopped road, shrugged off the effects of the rain and got down to the serious business of enjoying themselves. They were aided and abetted by the privileged members of the press that Court had seen fit to include in the entourage.

After the first half hour, Drew was the only one in the room unmoved by the euphoric party atmosphere. He attributed his lack of enthusiasm to the preparations he'd had to make, the week he'd spent overseeing the cleaning crew, searching for a catering service willing to do the party on such short notice in such an unlikely location, then constructing a makeshift board walkway from the road to the hotel doorway so that the ladies could get out of the cars and not sink ankle-deep into mud. His dark mood couldn't have anything to do with the fact that he felt as if he were setting Diana Powell up for a fall. In one way or another.

He hadn't seen her since the decision had been made to give her the job. He'd notified her by phone of Bernice Foods' acceptance of her bid. When he'd arrived at the saloon earlier, Court had informed him that Diana and her friend were upstairs changing. Drew had raised an eyebrow and asked if he was planning a party or an unveiling. Court had said, "a little of both," and smiled in a way Drew didn't like.

He knew too well his boss's ability to charm as well as terrorize. Court, long divorced from a mercenary woman, had nevertheless a hunting instinct when it came to the female of the species, and he wasn't averse to using his position and wealth to enhance the trap. Which member of the female species was Court hunting tonight? He'd admired Diana on the videotape. Did he intend to do more than admire her? And if he did, how would the vulnerable Diana react to a high-powered man like Courtney? Would she see the advantage of having a personal relationship with Court and jump through his hoop to take that advantage?

Drew drummed his fingers on the bar. From his post beside the curve of gleaming mahogany, the stairs were in full view as they emerged from the overhang of the ceiling. Diana hadn't yet come down. What was taking the lady so long?

In the upstairs hotel room that Court had said she and Jeanine could use, the lady was trying to decide what to wear. She'd brought two dresses, but she hadn't put either of them on. Dressed in her black lingerie and embroidered hose, she clipped around the splintery floor in her high heels, trying to ignore the nervous flutter in her stomach and the tendency her hands had to shake, convincing herself all the while that she had nothing to worry about.

"I'm charging double time for my services tonight," Jeanine said crisply. "Getting duded up for this party is above and beyond the call of duty."

Diana turned to look at her friend.

Grumbling every minute, Jeanine had stripped out of her jeans and donned a silky green dress that matched her eyes and made her hair look like spun silk. She felt more at home in denims and a sweatshirt and she'd said so. More than once.

"I'm sorry you have to dress up." With a hand that shook, Diana tossed her blusher and mascara into the makeup bag that gaped open on top of the dresser, making it teeter on its unsturdy legs. "But I'm not sorry you're here. And you have nothing to worry about. You look lovely."

"I'm not the lovely type. I'm the loyal type." Voices and laughter seeped up from downstairs, the bareness of the wood floor and the emptiness of the room amplifying the sounds. "They don't need us down there. Can't we slip down the back stairs, jump on our horses and ride away?"

"Number one, we don't have horses. Number two, if you think I'm going downstairs to face that crowd alone, you're wrong."

Jeanine ran a brush through her straight, blond hair, which fell in a curve under her chin. "Is it the crowd you don't want to face? Or a man who stands six-two and looks like Jason wearing his golden fleece?"

"I'm not afraid of Drew Lindstrom."

"But are you afraid of what you might feel for him, given half a chance?"

Diana turned to gaze at Jeanine. "Are you changing your tune?"

Jeanine's eyes shifted away. "I have to admit I was wrong about the guy. He didn't make a move on you, but you still got the contract."

"He got what he wanted from me."

Jeanine raised an eyebrow.

Diana tossed the brush on the dresser and drew up the side of her hair with a decorative comb. "As we say in the business world, he needed a warm body. I fit the bill. I don't think I need to worry about Mr. Lindstrom anymore, unless his charming cousin-in-law reappears on the scene."

"Are you sure about that?"

"I'm sure."

"So." Jeanine's eyes flickered to the two dresses hanging on the wall hook. "Which dress are you going to wear? Safe? Or sensational?"

FOR DREW, Diana's descent behind Jeanine into the noisy crowd was agonizingly slow. When she reached the bottom and stepped fully into the light, he muttered an oath and rammed his hands into his pants pockets to keep them from curling into fists. The gown she wore bared shoulder and knee with equal daring, and what wasn't exposed was hugged in loving detail. Never mind Boston. That dress should be banned worldwide.

Before Drew could move toward her, Court's head lifted like that of a lion scenting his prey. Effortlessly he detached himself from the little knot of people gathered around him and glided toward the women. Drew stopped where he was, took a step backward and resumed his slouch against the bar, watching.

Was it Drew's imagination, or did Diana look apprehensive rather than delighted at the sight of Court bearing down on her? Or was Drew superimposing qualities on her he wished she possessed? For a while after he'd left Rock Falls, he'd found himself doing that, endowing the women who caught his interest with Jamie's integrity. He'd soon learned to stop living in a dreamworld.

The noise seemed to assault Diana in waves. She felt detached, displaced. A tucked shirtfront surrounded by a black evening jacket loomed in front of her, and Diana looked up into Courtney Hughes's eyes. They gleamed with a wicked, masculine appreciation.

"Ms Powell." He bowed over her hand with an old-world courtliness that seemed strangely right for him. "How nice to see you in full battle dress."

Treacherous man, to treat her like royalty and then toss her a one-line zinger. He'd seen right through her. There was nothing left for her to do but carry it off as best she could. "You're very impressive yourself, Mr. Hughes." And how true that was. Dressed in a tuxedo, he was a formidable sight. "Have you met my friend, Jeanine Lacey?"

"I don't believe I've had the pleasure." His eyes assessed shrewdly, while Jeanine's glittered with defiance.

"Jeanine is also my bookkeeper and project assistant. She'll be working with me closely on the renovation."

"I see. A friend who's on the payroll. What could be more convenient?"

At the lightly veiled insult, Jeanine paled. Diana spoke up. "For me, certainly, but not for her. There are weeks when she gets her salary in peanut butter."

An elegant dark eyebrow rose. "Really?"

"Yes, really. There are some weeks when even the peanut butter is in short supply—"

"Diana." Jeanine frowned and shook her head warningly. "We don't need to share all our...secrets with Mr. Hughes. He is, after all, employing us."

Court smiled. "Your friend is trying to protect you. Loyal through and through. I'm intrigued by her tenacity. I thought it was an unknown quality among good-looking women. Ms Lacey?"

Court offered his arm to Jeanine with such assurance that she, looking stunned, took it. He gave his other to Diana, and as if it were his divine right, began to circle the room with the two of them, making introductions.

Diana had to put aside her worries about Jeanine and concentrate on the people Court was presenting to them. They met a John and a Mark and a Paul. John was short and balding and a member of the Bernice board; Mark had the prairie-toughened and uncom-

promisingly honest look of a South Dakota rancher;
Paul was with the press. So far, so good.

Court handed both her and Jeanine a glass of champagne, made a great show of toasting them and
watched Jeanine with hooded eyes while she tasted the
bubbling wine. Seeing that look, Diana's throat went
dry, and she drank hers more quickly then she should
have.

She continued to sip as he steered both of them toward a group of women clustered around a green-
baized table. Ann, Helen and Mary were added to the
list. Then there were Kevin and Kim and Evan. One
more rhyming name and she was going to forget the
entire bunch.

"You two are doing very well." She was on her second glass of the bubbly when Court took pity on them,
steered them to one side and handed them each an ap-
petizer on a white napkin that bore the Bernice logo in
the corner. The pastry was hot and delicious, phyllo
dough wrapped around steaming crab. Diana had a
feeling it was too late to cut the effect of the alcohol. She
was already lightheaded.

"Like it?" Court inquired.

"I love hot crab. Speaking of which, where's Mr.
Lindstrom?"

Court nearly spilt his drink and for the first time that
evening, Jeanine's smile was spontaneous.

"I believe you'll find him over by the bar. Shall I send
word for him to join us?" At the startled look on her
face, Court added, "Or were you merely curious?"

"As you say, I was just . . . wondering." Diana's gid-
diness moved a notch higher on the Richter scale. She'd
had very little to eat all day; her stomach had been too
tight with anticipation.

A waiter approached Court and stood holding a tray. He reached for another hors d'oeuvre impaled on a toothpick. "Try this one. Perhaps you'll like the cold shrimp and egg as much as you did the hot crab." His eyes gleaming with amusement, he held it up to Diana's mouth. Why was it she had this feeling that she shouldn't be humoring him? He looked exactly like a man holding four aces back-to-back. She nibbled the food off the pick, took a sip of champagne to banish the salty taste and watched as Court's gaze wandered over her shoulder to Jeanine's face. Her friend looked strangely flushed.

"Well?" He sounded amused.

"Every bit as good," Diana said, knowing she was out of her league. Courtney was playing a game with her, but only he knew the reason why.

As if she were a child who'd successfully completed an assignment, he gave her a benevolent smile and took both her and Jeanine by the arms again, guiding them across the room to introduce yet another man who belonged to the Bernice Food organization. The man's eyes skimmed over Jeanine and then flashed to Diana, roaming over her with something close to dislike in them. Pretending at civility, he asked her how she'd gotten into the construction business.

"I'm following in my mother's footsteps," she said straight-faced, and flashed him a hundred-watt smile while she lifted her glass to her lips. Court laughed. "I'm leaving you in excellent hands, Burns. Excuse Ms Lacey and me, won't you?" The look he gave Jeanine was strange, almost conciliatory. Jeanine's face looked even stranger. She seemed angry yet helpless to say so. Without another word, Court put a firm hand on Jeanine's back and steered her away. Diana watched them go, wondering if she was throwing Jeanine to the wolf.

Distracted, she turned back to find the unpleasant little man looking at her expectantly. "And how long have you been with Bernice Foods, Mr....Brown?" Yes, his name was Brown. B as in Bernice Foods. Or was it Black?

The man gave her an annoyed stare. "My name is Burns, Ms Powell."

"Oh, yes. I beg your pardon. You aren't by any chance the Burns of the Burns and Stalker Study of 1961, the study that recommends matching organization to technology, are you?"

The chilliness of his stare dropped three more degrees. "I'm part of Mr. Hughes's staff. As I believe he mentioned to you. Do you have problems with retention, Ms Powell? I should think that a person in management would be skilled at remembering small details."

She *was* skilled at remembering small details. It was just that, at the moment, that particular skill was floating under two glasses of champagne, very little food and a supreme consciousness of the blond man who stood leaning against the bar watching her. Not moving. Just—watching.

"I'm quite skilled at recalling small details, Mr. Burns." To hide her nervousness, she lifted the champagne glass to her mouth. A hand caught her elbow in midair, pulling the glass down, and a smooth masculine voice drawled from somewhere above her left ear, "Excuse us for a moment, Ned, won't you? I need a word with Ms Powell."

Burns looked at the glass that Drew had thrust at him—Diana's—and then at Diana with equal disdain.

With an insistent hand at her back, Drew escorted her with slightly more enthusiasm than she thought necessary through a rear door and out into the cool May night, where he brought her to a stop under a porch overhang that protected them from the light mist that was still falling.

"Ned. His name is Ned. If he'd told me that, I wouldn't have had so much trouble remembering who he was. I once had a dog named Ned, and he didn't like me, either. What is Mr. Burn's problem?"

"He's a teetotaling misogynist."

"I must have made a wonderful impression on him."

"You don't have to impress him or anybody else. You've got the contract."

She should have been comforted by his words. She wasn't. He sounded cool, indifferent, removed. Diana inhaled deeply, trying to think logically. But it was hard to be logical on a night like this, when the breeze whispered secrets and the night clouds glowed.

Only after the soft, moist breeze brushed across Drew's face did he realize he'd done something he hadn't done since Jamie. He'd acted to protect a woman. He'd watched Diana sipping champagne and smiling that high-powered smile of hers, and he'd watched Court introduce her to Burns and walk away with what looked to be the new blonde who was ready to fall into Court's rabbit hutch. And he'd known instinctively that Diana was teetering on the edge of trouble.

She was a bright, beautiful lady. She didn't need his protection. He slid his hand away from her and sliced it through his hair, wondering what had possessed him to interfere. His policy was live and let live.

Turning his back to Diana, Drew faced into the night. Beyond loomed the slanting canyon walls that gave

Shadow Gap its name. The rain clouds glistened with an odd metallic sheen. The heavy moistness in the air brought her scent drifting to his nose, something light and French and totally hers. He tensed his shoulders to resist the night that whispered sensual secrets, the scent she wore that invited him to explore those secrets.

Feeling uneasy, Diana stood looking at his back, wondering if she'd ever seen Drew's spine quite that straight. The way he looked in that chocolate-brown tux with his hands thrust into his pockets was a crime and a sin—so golden haired, so easy moving, so unaware of his potency. Whatever his feelings were at being alone with her now, a moment ago he'd acted to protect her. She owed him thanks for that. And for fairly considering her bid. Before she lost her nerve, she said, "I want to thank you."

He didn't turn around. He stood where he was—a tall, unbending man with something on his mind. "What for?"

"For not giving in to your prejudices about my company."

He twisted around suddenly, making her start with surprise. His face was shadowed, but Diana could feel his indifference leave him as if he'd flung it away. "You don't owe me any thanks." His voice was hard. "I recommended that the bid be given to another company. It was Court who acted as your standard-bearer. He was so impressed by your performance on the videotape that he insisted you be given the bid." He paused, and in the dark she could almost feel his eyes moving over her. "From the way you smiled at him, I thought you'd guessed what happened."

Feeling disturbed and more hurt than she should have, she took a step toward him. "I was sure you'd had a change of heart. How silly of me." She took a breath. "I wonder why you work so diligently at believing the worst of me."

His body posture was lazy, relaxed. "I don't have to work at it. You make it easy by being so obvious."

"How am I obvious?"

He stepped forward a little and looked at her, taking his time, letting his gaze run over her bare shoulders and the provocative fit of her dress. "You're bright enough to know that if Court finds you attractive enough to take to bed, he won't be so eager to sue if you don't bring the job in on time. You took out a little insurance and came dressed looking available, hoping he'd succumb. Your little scheme worked beautifully. You baited him and left him wriggling on the hook."

She would have laughed at the image of Court Hughes on a hook if Drew's words hadn't hurt her so badly. "The agility of your mind amazes me. But as long as you're assigning me nefarious schemes, why have me stop with Mr. Hughes? Why shouldn't I include you in my itinerary of scheduled seductions . . . for insurance purposes?"

He took another step closer and said in a low, dark voice, "I don't know. I only know that you haven't . . . and it's a damn shame."

He was looking at her, his face dark, his golden hair silvered in the faint light. She said, "You think so?"

"I know so." He took a step closer, and she was in his arms. He stood holding her, one hand coming up to pluck the comb out of her hair, bringing the dark strands tumbling down around her ears. Stunned by the sensual spell of his hands, she felt boneless. He went on holding her, looking down into her moonlit eyes. Wanting, needing to understand, she said, "If I'm the kind of woman you say I am, why do you want to hold me?"

"I can't help myself." Amusement flavored his voice. She moved to push him away; he stopped her. "Wouldn't you rather hear that than be told how beautiful you are?"

She stopped trying to push him away and stood staring at him. "You are a dangerous man. You know entirely too much about women."

"I'm a pussycat compared to Court."

"I wasn't flirting with him."

"Weren't you? He had you eating out of his hand, in more ways than one."

"He was being polite, and so was I." She tried to think of the words that would convince him. She couldn't. His face was changing subtly, taking on that look a man wore when he looked at a woman he wanted. His breathing had altered, too. Or was it hers?

"I suppose it doesn't matter much now. Court's chosen the charming blonde."

"Then all your warnings have been wasted, haven't they?" She felt breathless, deprived of air.

"I'm only trying to keep you from getting hurt. You're such a . . . You should have learned long ago that it doesn't pay to be polite to stalking cougars."

"So I'm finding out," she murmured, her eyes on him.

A long beat of silence went by. Then he said, "I'm not stalking you, Diana."

"I know you aren't—" her chin came up "—and it's a damn shame."

In the breathless, heart-stopping silence that followed, she was afraid he wouldn't take her blatant invitation.

With a deliberate grace, he covered her mouth with
his. But as their mouths met, the cynicism, the mockery disappeared. His mobile mouth softened, warmed,
moved to take her in, to possess without hurting her,
to cherish without smothering her. This Drew was
without pretense, and her heart soared. He made her
hungry and fed her at the same time, his kiss a primi-
tive claiming of her mouth. Her body responded, her
heart pulsing in her throat, her abdomen tightening. He
broke the kiss before her thirst was sated, but as if he
still needed to touch her, with a hand at her nape, he
guided her head to his chest, where she felt the accelerated beat of his heart.

"Stay away from Court. He eats women like you."

She lifted her head. "And you won't?"

He slid his hand slowly, suggestively down her spine,
and then he released her. She felt chilled by his absence
but she knew instinctively that he needed the space to
regain his composure. For so did she. "It's too soon to
tell whether you'll give me the power to hurt you or
not."

Her chin came up. "I'd be a fool if I did."

"Would you?" The question was heavy with sensuality. "Still think I'm interested in someone else?"

"You haven't denied it."

Drew leaned away from her, and with his character-
istic lazy ease, crossed his arms in front of him. "You
haven't asked for a denial. You pronounced me guilty
without trial."

She took a step toward him. "Was I wrong?"

"I'll let you decide." With loose-limbed ease, he
moved toward her, lifted a hand and dragged a careless finger along the top of her dress. He was playing a
game with her. She knew that, but it took all the con-

trol she had to stand unmoving under that deliberately intimate caress. "Would I touch you like this if I loved another woman?"

She was breathless. "Perhaps…if you were sure there was no hope of your love being returned."

His mouth tightened, but he made no reply. He raised his hand a bit to find and trace her collarbone, the vee of her throat. When she made no move to stop him, he trailed his hand to her opposite shoulder, in a caress that made her skin flame.

"My God," he said, "I've been wanting to do that all night. And it feels better than I imagined it would. It feels good for you, too, doesn't it? Tell me it does."

His palm slid on a path downward, over satin skin and taffeta, until he was cupping her breast. "Tell me, Diana."

Her throat was dry. "Yes," she breathed. "Yes."

He brought her closer, locking her hips to his. His hand lifted higher, sculpting the jut of her chin, climbing to her mouth. His thumb caught her lower lip, tugged sensuously, asking for entrance. She allowed it, moistening him with her tongue. Instantly his mouth replaced his hand, his tongue flicking at hers, probing with the same lazy sensuality his thumb had. He showed her what making love with him would be like, tiny, stinging surprises of taste, touch and texture orchestrated solely to pleasure her. And there was more.

His palm brushed down her spine from nape to buttock, making the taffeta rustle and slide against her hips. He pulled her body against his, letting her feel the evidence of his desire for her. Every nerve in her abdomen leaped to life, tingling with the beginning of need. His hands still cupping her buttocks in that shockingly intimate way, he lifted his mouth, his smile dark, lazy, inviting. "If we don't rejoin the others soon, we won't go back at all. Which is it to be, Diana?"

Diana ached to leave the party with him. And couldn't. His heart was in another woman's keeping. Strange how she forgot that when she was in his arms. Physically at least, he held back nothing. For one shining moment he had made her feel as if she were the only woman in the world.

She went up on tiptoe and brushed his mouth in helpless despair, once, twice, three times, wanting him desperately to understand. But on each pass, she knew she was living in a dreamworld. His mouth was far too enticing. If she didn't step out of his arms soon, she'd want to stay there. Not for a night but forever. She pushed at him carefully, asking for release before she lost the will to leave his arms.

"I don't think I've ever been told no quite so nicely."

His words were bland. He hadn't been hurt by her refusal because she meant nothing to him. She'd aroused his body but not his mind. Or his heart. That belonged to Jamie.

"We'd better go in." She'd done the right thing. But why did the right thing hurt so badly?

5

WHEN THEY RETURNED to the brilliantly lit saloon, Diana hid her confused emotions behind a bright smile. Now if she moved away from Drew, she just might survive.

He didn't allow it. He handed her a glass of champagne and pushed her gently onto a bar stool, her back against the bar. When she obeyed his unspoken command, he remained standing, leaning against the bar, his hip against her thigh, his mouth curved in that devastating smile. As if he hardly knew she existed, he struck up a conversation with the man on his right.

Diana worked desperately to recover her poise. But how could she while her body sang with the memory of his? Her hands remembered his silken hair, and her mouth stung with the knowledge that his was as sexy as that sensual fullness had promised.

To make matters worse, as they'd made their way into the saloon, they'd met Jeanine and Court on their way out into the moist, dark night. Court's hand was on Jeanine's back, and he wore the expression of a man in pursuit. Jeanine's face was flushed. They were obviously seeking the privacy of the porch.

She should have done something to save Jeanine, Diana thought. But what? Grabbed her hand and warned her not to follow any man into that dangerous South Dakota mist? Jeanine was old enough to know what she was doing. Or was she? Was "old enough to know better" a mythical age that no woman ever reached when a man was involved?

Obviously, Diana hadn't reached it yet. She was sitting there as docilely as a lamb, willingly torturing herself by sitting so close to Drew that she could see him fit the champagne glass to his lips every time he drank.

As if he sensed her thoughts, he turned his head and threw a careless, mocking smile at her.

Her own mouth lifted, and suddenly, so did her heart. Drew's smile deepened, and he raised his champagne glass to her in a salute that was sheer charm. Swallowing, Diana moved her hips slightly, trying to find a more secure perch on the stool.

She sat there with her eyes locked onto his until he turned away. Only then did her skin finally stop tingling from the effect of Drew's glance, and her thoughts turn to what he'd told her out there under the dripping eaves. He hadn't approved of her being given the bid. He'd voted against her.

A few days ago, Shadow Gap had been nothing more to her than an interesting job. Now it was a glove thrown down, a gauntlet to run. She had to prove she was capable of bringing the project in on time. Was it possible to fail? Anxiety took up permanent residence inside her.

Before, she'd tried champagne as an antidote to her nerves and that had gotten her into trouble. This time she sipped slowly and carefully. Suppose she couldn't do it? Suppose she hadn't organized the job well enough? Suppose her materials didn't come when they should? Suppose a foundation proved to be more unstable than it had seemed, and the specs hadn't called for enough work and materials. Suppose it rained for six weeks solidly. Suppose the sky should fall or there was an earthquake—*Stop it, Diana. You're being ridiculous, and you know it.*

She was being ridiculous. She didn't want to feel edgy, as though her reputation was on the line. But it was. If she couldn't be the woman Drew loved, she wanted desperately to be the woman he respected.

When the limousines that Court had hired arrived to take the guests back to their accommodations in Hot Springs, Diana was given something new to worry about. Jeanine, looking flushed and more than a little off balance, was shepherded gently onto a plush seat next to Court. At the last minute, she turned and sketched a wave at Diana. Helplessly, anxiously, Diana waved back. Jeanine was a grown woman. But was she grown enough to handle Courtney Hughes?

At her side, Drew said in a low voice, "Your friend seems to have taken my place in the limo. I'll need a ride back. Have a seat at the bar and wait for me. I'll drive."

He wasn't her employer, but he certainly took on the role easily enough. "It's not necessary for you to drive. I'm perfectly capable of—"

"Fine, you drive." She'd been braced for an argument. "Either way, you have to wait for me."

He escorted her to the bar, half lifting her up onto the seat. Needing to distract herself from the feel of his warm fingers on her bare flesh, she said, "You do have this bad habit of letting your transportation get away from you."

He smiled that maddening, lazy smile that promised so much and delivered nothing. "Yes, don't I?"

The catering crew quickly packed away glasses, food and liquor. Too quickly. In moments they had loaded their van and left, leaving Drew and Diana alone again under the dark sky. The mist had stopped, but the clouds remained. Moisture hung in the air, heavy, sensual, reminiscent of their time together on the porch.

Without asking, he extended his hand for the keys. Without protesting, she gave them to him.

Inside the car, the dash lights illuminated his chiseled, closed face. He might have been made of the same granite as the hills. She tore her gaze away from him and looked out into the forest darkness. Some fatalistic urge, brought to bubbling life by too much champagne and the memory of his touch, made her say, "Tell me about your cousin. How did he meet his wife?"

Drew's lips curled in an ironic smile. "Jamie was an elementary teacher just as I was. She had his daughter in class."

"So your cousin went to a parent-teacher association meeting and thought he'd conduct his own parent-teacher merger?"

Drew smiled; he couldn't help himself. The woman was pushing, and he found he liked her in this mood—reckless, daring. He'd like her even more if she were reckless and daring in bed beside him. It had taken all the control he had to release her from that kiss on the porch, to walk inside and protect her from Court's speculation and Burns's as well, by pretending that it had never happened. "It wasn't that easy. Blake didn't meet her until he was released."

That brought her head up. "Released . . . as from prison?"

"Released, as from terrorists. He was held hostage overseas for six months. You must have heard something about it."

"I suppose I did. But I didn't connect the name. And no one said anything at the dinner. . . ."

"Blake sees to that. He's not interested in rehashing the past." There was a silence in the car. "Particularly since he married Jamie."

Diana thought Drew had said all he was going to say, but then he went on, "It was difficult for them. Blake had a scar on his face and a few in his head. It took a woman like Jamie to bring him out of his shell."

"I see." The Lindstrom cousins were more alike than they recognized. And Jamie was the kind of woman who would be equally adept at delving beneath Drew's smooth facade of lazy indifference. But Jamie hadn't chosen the handsome, charming cousin. She'd chosen the difficult one with the scar.

"I take it the course of true love didn't run smooth."

"Not smooth . . . but straight."

He drove around the hairpin curves of the mountain road carefully at first, then accelerated slightly. Diana's spirit of daring was infecting him. He wanted to feel her body slam into his, feel her softness against his hardness. But there was a console between them, and she clung to the door as if her life depended on it. Perhaps it did.

He couldn't pursue her now, not while she believed he was in love with Jamie. He had to bide his time, let her begin the renovation of Shadow Gap and get a good chunk of the work under her belt. He'd shaken her confidence out there on the porch—he knew that. He shouldn't have told her he wasn't responsible for her getting the bid. But she was so damn honest with him, how could he be any less so with her?

The gods were meting out his punishment now. He had to let her alone. He couldn't muddle the issue by pursuing her. There would be time for that later. Meanwhile he would have to live with this ever-tightening feeling in his gut that grew worse every time he looked at her. He wanted to taste more of her, touch more of her. But he couldn't. Not yet.

When he braked to a stop, he turned in his seat to face her. "I'll have Les return your car in the morning."

"At six o'clock, please."

He raised an eyebrow. "That will give you—" he glanced at his watch "—exactly four hours' sleep."

She looked at him and said in a low, clear voice, "I have work to do. And—" she took a breath "—I doubt if I'll be sleeping much tonight."

Her honesty jolted him into blunt honesty of his own. "Because you're worried about the project...or because I kissed you?"

"Yes," she said.

There was a silence. His arm, stretched along the back of the seat, brought his hand too near. She had a sudden urge to lay her cheek against it. Disturbed by her thoughts, she tried to move away and discovered he had caught a lock of her hair.

"I want you to succeed. You believe that, don't you?"

"Are you defending yourself?"

"Against you?" he murmured. "If I am, I don't have a snowball's chance in hell of pulling it off." Slowly he released his hold on her hair.

Shaken, Diana pulled her shawl around her shoulders and climbed out of the car to walk into the dark, whispery night and the waiting trailer.

She was still awake twenty minutes later when a key rattled in the door lock. Startled, she lay quiet, tense. A familiar head loomed in the open door, and a familiar French scent filled the trailer as Jeanine stepped in. Stealthily, shoes in hand, she crept toward the bunk.

"You didn't stay long."

The shoes fell to the floor. Letting out a resigned sigh, Jeanine reached for the switch. Light flooded the small trailer, making both women blink. "I was hoping you'd be asleep."

Diana raised herself up on one elbow. "Is he as high-powered personally as he is professionally?"

Jeanine turned away, her blond hair falling over her cheek, concealing it from Diana's view. "I wouldn't know. Nor do I care."

"You mean he didn't—"

"Oh, yes, we went to his hotel suite. But when he made it clear that he wanted—" her head came up "—that he was sure I would climb into the sack with him the minute I walked in the door, I told him I wanted to leave. So he called his chauffeur to bring me home in the limo."

"And now you wonder if you made a mistake."

"No, I don't," Jeanine said fiercely. She turned away and began to get ready for bed, shrugging out of the green dress and tossing it aside, as if by doing so she could cast away the memories of the evening.

"Didn't you expect that when you went with him?"

Jeanine faced her. "You're going to kill yourself laughing. But no, I didn't. The cool, with-it, been-around-the-block-twice kid didn't expect to be tossed into the sack as if she were the bed tray he meant to eat his dinner off. I should have known better. I was a fool to think all he wanted was to talk. But we'd had an interesting conversation and there had been so many people around that I thought it would be like a scaled-down party, and I—Oh, hell, why bother making excuses. Maybe I did want to go to bed with him but not . . . like that. Not as if I were his Saturday midnight snack. I was a fool." Clad in her cotton nightshirt, she plopped down on the bunk and cast Diana a rueful look. "Never thought I'd be caught playing the part of the cockeyed optimist. That's your role, not mine."

Relieved that her sense of humor was reasserting itself, Diana smiled. "It happens to the best of us."

"Not to me, it doesn't. Not again. Not ever again." Jeanine snapped off the light. Lying there listening to her crawl into her bunk, Diana wondered if Katharine Hepburn was right when she said that perhaps men and women should live next door to each other and just visit occasionally.

6

IN THE EARLY-MORNING HOURS of the day Diana was to start work on Shadow Gap, the town was vandalized. The destroyers came with saws, sledgehammers and gallons of obnoxious, deep green paint. They used the hammers on the back side of the Fargo building, smashing most of the remaining authentic boards. They used saws on the delicate spindle trim around the porch of W. Oliver's house until nothing was left but toothpicks. The green paint they slathered around the inside of the schoolhouse in great gobs. The walls, the ceiling, the floor, the blackboards, the oak bookcase, the teacher's desk—nothing escaped the paint can.

Diana stared at the damage, wanting desperately not to believe what her eyes were telling her. Beside her, Jeanine gripped her hand. "I know what you're thinking, but you can't do it. You can't clean this up without letting anyone know. You've got to call Lindstrom and renegotiate the contract. The company was responsible for the town's security until you rolled onto the site this morning."

Diana took a deep breath, trying to think. "He expected me to be incompetent and ask for more time. How quickly I'm going to live up to his expectations." She smiled ruefully.

"This isn't your fault," Jeanine said fiercely. "It's unprofessional not to call him. And stupid. If you won't do it, I will. What's his number?"

Diana shook her head. Jeanine was right. It was un-professional—and emotional—not to call Drew. But she would have given a large sum of money if she could have avoided it. "No, it's my job. I'll do it." She sighed, thinking of the long, hot drive back to the campsite. She hadn't had a telephone line installed in Shadow Gap yet.

Could she pick up the phone and tell Drew, in a calm, businesslike voice, what had happened? That was precisely what she had to do, and immediately. He'd returned to Boston on an early flight yesterday. She only hoped he was at the office. Given the time difference, he should be.

The trailer was already heating from the sun when she returned to pull open the door and drop down beside the telephone. Her fingers trembled as she dialed the 555 exchange and the number of the Bernice Foods office.

She remembered the receptionist and Drew's secretary and, from the sound of their voices, they remembered her. To her surprise, she was put through immediately.

His drawl brought the heat up under her skin. "Trouble, Diana?"

"Yes. There's been vandalism at the site."

He was silent for a moment. She tensed, waiting for his response. "How bad?"

"Boards smashed on the Fargo building, ginger-bread trim demolished on the banker's house and green paint splashed all over the inside of the schoolhouse."

His muttered curse echoed her feelings exactly. "Nothing done to the hotel?"

"No. They either guessed about the alarm or ran out of time."

"Any sign of how they gained entrance?"

"The fence was cut. That will have to be repaired, too. And I'll have to post twenty-four-hour security, a cost I didn't factor into the original bid."

Drew said another succinct, heartfelt word. "Don't touch a thing. I'll catch the first available plane out of here to verify the damage."

At her silence, he said, "I believe you, Diana. But verification is routine; you know that."

She did know it. But she hadn't expected him to drop everything and come flying back to South Dakota. She'd expected him to send someone else.

His voice came over the line, brisk and businesslike. "Give me your number and stay by the phone. I'll call you back as soon as I've made my travel arrangements so you'll know when and where to meet me. See if you can find somebody with a camera to take pictures."

"Jeanine's already done that."

"Good for her. Sit tight. I'll get right back to you."

The when of his arrival turned out to be three o'clock that afternoon. The where was Rapid City. He'd take a charter from Sioux Falls in order to get there as quickly as possible.

THE SUN WAS HIGH and hot in the sky when he climbed out of the plane and strode across the field of the airport toward her, carrying his briefcase and a canvas carryall. In his brown pinstripe, he looked as if he'd just stepped out of his office. It was the first time she'd seen him dressed in the uniform of a businessman. He did extraordinary things to a suit, his tall lean figure moving gracefully inside the cloth, his hair blowing in the prairie wind. "Hello, blue eyes."

With the careless ease she remembered so well, he cupped one hand on her shoulder and brushed his lips over her forehead as if he greeted her that way every day of the week. "This isn't the end of the world. Paint can be removed; boards can be replaced." At her dazed relief, he flashed her a grin. "That's better. You got out of that car looking as if your dog had died."

Diana wanted to hit him or kiss him—she wasn't sure which would give her the most satisfaction. Before she could decide, he'd tossed his carryall into the trunk and slid into the passenger seat.

It shouldn't have been such a relief to see him. It was. It shouldn't have felt so good sitting beside him in the car again, breathing his scent. It did. She hadn't expected his instant understanding. But how good it felt to have him spread reassurance over her like honey.

Drew cursed mentally. Why had things gone wrong the minute she was scheduled to take over? He'd known from her voice on the phone how she'd hated to call him. Now that he was here, he could see how hard she was taking it. Her usual vitality was gone. She looked bruised under the eyes. He'd joked with her to stop himself from pulling her close and kissing the life out of her. Damn it, the town was just a job, not a life-or-death project. He stared out the window, thinking that a week ago he couldn't have thought that. The town had been his obsession for more than a year. And now it was hers.

An obsession they shared. Among other things. They shared a love for laughter and a love for old things that told the stories of people's lives, and a love for touching....

Not a pleasant thought to have when he was sitting so close to her in the ancient car she drove, so close that he could see her breasts lift under her cotton shirt. Couldn't the woman have the common courtesy to look unattractive in work clothes? No. In her plaid cotton shirt and jeans, belted in to an impossibly small waist, she looked sexy as hell. He hadn't been sorry to whip into Court's office, explain the situation and have Court's growled acquiescence to his travel arrangements, knowing he would see her again far sooner than he'd planned.

He tried to crank down Sam's window on his side of the ancient car and discovered it didn't work. "All the modern conveniences."

"I'm sorry. Sam is old and cranky."

"It doesn't matter. I'll rent a car tomorrow. Did you contact the police?"

In the heat, he loosened his tie and unbuttoned his jacket. Diana clutched the wheel a little more tightly. The man was stripping down in her front seat, pulling his tie out from under his collar and unbuttoning his shirt.

He shed his suit coat and tossed it into her back seat. As he turned toward her, she caught a glimpse of a patch of blond hair at the base of his throat. He was staying long enough to rent a car? How long would that be? She couldn't ask. "Yes."

"What did they say?"

"That they'd investigate."

Drew grunted, reminding her of his father, Thad. "Big of them. Was the fence cut with wire clippers?"

"Yes."

"So it wasn't just a bunch of kids out to impress one another."

She'd been so sure that was the answer. "Couldn't kids have wire cutters?"

"I suppose they could. But it definitely requires malice aforethought."

On the plane, he'd had time to think about that. Paint inside the schoolroom, boards damaged on the Fargo building and the trim shredded on the banker's house. It was as if the vandals knew exactly where to cause the most damage. The only place they'd missed was the hotel. Court had had the foresight to have an alarm system installed there before the party. Drew had chided Court for his caution, saying such precautions weren't necessary on the South Dakota prairie. How wrong he'd been.

As they walked through the town looking at the damage, Drew cursed under his breath. At the Fargo building, Diana pushed her hair out of her eyes and straightened her shoulders, working hard to look unmoved. At the banker's house, she stood very still in the weeds beside him while he stared at the denuded porch and the shredded, splintered triangular wedges of decorative trim that had originally nestled under the peaks. Her hands were clenched at her sides, and her face was pale. He wanted to say something to ease her pain. He couldn't think of a single damn word that would make her feel better.

The schoolhouse was worse than he'd thought it could be. Here, damage had been done that could not be undone without a great deal of paint remover and scrubbing. The blackboards, the floor, the ceiling, the stove, even the bookcase hadn't escaped. Worst of all, someone had smashed the glass of the oak case and smeared paint over the books inside.

Drew pivoted slowly, surveying the damage, his heart dropping. When he faced Diana, he realized he wasn't thinking of the damage so much as how desperately he wanted to ease her pain.

"Sixty years." Her voice was unsteady. "Sixty years this stood here undamaged, and now—"

He turned to her and opened his arms. Her eyes met his, and she saw the warmth, the empathetic pain. She flew to him, nuzzling her face into his shirt, instinctively seeking his comfort. His arms folded around her tightly, and she closed her eyes, locking out the sight of the room.

"It's all right, Diana." His voice was low, husky with an unmistakable throb of tenderness. "We'll find a way to—"

Her arms came up to encircle him, her fingers biting into his back. "There's no way we can undo this. The books—the books I loved so much are—"

He grasped her head in both hands and pulled her back, forcing her to look into his face. "No. We'll find a way." When she made a small sound of protest, he covered her mouth with his, fiercely giving her the softness, the sweetness, the sadness. She kissed him back, greedily taking the succor he offered. As tender as he'd been fierce, he lifted his mouth to her eyes and kissed away her tears. "We'll get paint remover and we'll sand and varnish," he murmured between kisses. "And we'll find someone who can restore the books."

She lifted her head, her smile one part helpless laughter and one part tears. "It's so romantic to be kissed by a man while he's talking about paint remover and varnish."

Drew's smile was lazy, self-assured, breathtaking. "Make up your mind, woman. What do you want, romance or help?" His eyes gleamed as he waited for her answer.

"I want . . . help, of course."

His sea-green eyes darkened. "The ever-practical Diana. You're not very good for my ego."

"I . . . think we've been over this ground before." He was warm and hard, a masculine complement to her femininity, and it felt so good to be in his arms again. She was glad to see him. Too glad.

Diana pushed at him, asking for release. He let her go slowly, looking as reluctant to take his warmth away as she was to be separated from him.

He stood for a moment, his eyes and face unreadable. "I'll do the best I can with Court to get you as much extra money and time as you need."

Her head lifted. "I can't ask for anymore than that."

"What do you think?" His eyes moved over her face. "Five extra weeks' grace on the completion date, a thousand dollars to pay the guard and reimbursement for the extra supplies?"

"I don't want any concessions just because—"

"Just because what, Diana? Just because we exchanged a kiss?" A flash of temper brightened his eyes, only to be tamped down by his slow smile. "I don't come that cheap." His smile returned, deepening, carving deep, attractive lines on each side of his mouth. "Although I am open to negotiation—"

"Drew. Don't put this on a personal basis."

"As I recall, you were the one who brought up the question of concessions exchanged for kisses. I was making what I thought to be a reasonable adjustment."

"And it is," said Diana quickly. "I'll take it."

"Well. We agree on something at last. Better be careful, blue eyes. If this becomes a trend, we're in danger of becoming friends."

She smiled then; she couldn't help it. "That's a terrible risk to take."

"Some risks are worth it."

They were ambiguous words, provocative words. Diana spent the rest of the day trying to get them out of her head. But when she returned home with Jeanine, the mini crisis waiting for them banished thoughts of Drew's words. Their neighbor's trailer was smothered in boxes of long-stemmed red roses, and their neighbor was annoyed.

"That man said he had some flowers for you and could he leave them here. I said yes, expecting a little bitty bouquet like my husband gets for me once every ten years." Mrs. Sanderson's hands went to her hips. "I didn't expect to have so many boxes stacked into my trailer I couldn't move around to get supper."

"We're sorry, Mrs. Sanderson. Please, take a dozen to enjoy as our thanks."

Mrs. Sanderson looked slightly mollified. Diana moved to place a box in her hands. "Not that one," the woman objected. "That one's got the card in it." At Diana's raised brow, the older woman lifted her chin defiantly. "Well, naturally I was curious. Who wouldn't be?"

"Who, indeed?"

Trying very hard not to look satisfied with her booty, Mrs. Sanderson tucked the long white box under her arm and went inside her trailer. Jeanine piled another two boxes in Diana's arms, took one herself and unlocked the trailer door.

Inside, Jeanine turned eyes full of laughter up to Diana. "For heaven's sake, look at the card. 'Well, naturally I'm curious,'" she mimicked saucily. "Besides, I want to see what Drew Lindstrom has to say. He's certainly a fast worker. Making traveling plans, ordering flowers."

Diana reached into the box to dig out the card. One quick glance and her eyes sparkled with amusement. "I can't open the card."

"Diana, don't play games. Now now. I'll die of curiosity."

"You don't have to." Diana thrust the white card at Jeanine. "They're for you."

Her eyes wide, her smile fading, Jeanine held out her hand. "Me?" She looked down at the card as if it were a foreign object.

"Well?" Diana rocked back on her heels, her mouth twitching. "Open it. 'Naturally, I'm curious.'" But she wasn't curious, not really. She had a very good idea who'd sent Jeanine four dozen roses.

Jeanine raised a dazed face to Diana. "They're from Court. An apology."

"Imagine that." Diana tipped open the cover of the second box. "I'll see if I can find something to put them in. It's a good thing we gave Mrs. Sanderson a dozen." In the high voice of a spoiled Southern belle, à la Scarlett O'Hara, she added, "That boy certainly does know how to apologize. I do declare I don't know what he was thinking of." And in her own practical Iowa tone, "Or do I?"

TUESDAY, over Diana's protests, Drew began work on the schoolhouse.

Wednesday she contacted a company in California that dealt in trim for Victorian houses and ordered the twenty-five feet of spindle and running trim she needed for the Oliver house. They promised a six-week delivery date. The sawmill agreed to double her order of boards for the Fargo building.

By Friday, her success in recouping her losses was almost enough to make her forget that Drew had taken an apartment in the old brick hotel in Hot Springs and hadn't said when he planned to return to Boston.

Drew began the tedious work inside the schoolhouse, carefully applying paint remover and sander to the walls. During those next four weeks, he worked daily on the painstaking, backbreaking job. When he took his break and stood outside, drinking his cola, he watched the frenzy of activity generated by a brunette whirlwind. Wherever he looked on the construction site, Diana was there. She stood squaring her hands in front of the Cat, telling the operator to drop a pallet in the place she'd designated. When one of her employees grumbled about having to construct a burglar-proof shed to protect her supplies and house the telephone line she was having strung in, she shamed him into complying by wielding a hammer right alongside him. If there were errands to run, she didn't send others—she went herself. She was recreating his dream, and doing it with more speed and efficiency than he'd thought any human being capable of.

She wasn't just any human being. When he went home at night, lay down on the bed and closed his eyes, he seemed to see her on the back of his eyelids, dark glossy hair poking out from under the hard hat, her skin turning a golden brown from her exposure to the sun, her body sleek and trim.

He didn't need to work on the schoolhouse. He could go back to Boston. He should go back to Boston. Not because Court needed him in the city. Hughes had given him free rein on Shadow Gap, leaving the organization of his time to his own discretion. Drew told himself he was staying to see that the project went well, and that there was no more vandalism. But that wasn't the only reason he wanted to stay in South Dakota, and he knew it.

He certainly didn't need to look over Diana's shoulder. Yet every day he went out to the site, and every day he returned to the apartment he'd rented, his mood a mixture of contentment and frustration. Contentment that the work was going well. Frustration that arose from looking at Diana Powell.

If there was a weak link in the chain of her command, he didn't see it. During those first four weeks, her crew had jacked up the Fargo building and shored up the rubble foundations, as well as doing all the repairs to the other foundations. Other crew members had, under her direction, secured the site with fencing. A dumpster stood ready to receive trash.

During the next four weeks, Diana completed the outdoor structural renovation on the hotel and the schoolhouse. The subcontractors who'd been hired to do the plumbing were on site and working in the hotel, the building with first priority. The outdoor work on the Fargo building went more slowly.

DIANA WASN'T SLEEPING WELL. Nor was she eating well. She gulped vitamins and got in a jog occasionally, but she was conscious that time was sliding by at an ever-faster rate. She'd run into a few glitches, but nothing she hadn't been able to handle. The subcontractors were working smoothly on the site and managing, for the most part, to keep out of each other's way. She'd planned the whole thing like a ballet—outdoor men working on the Fargo building, plumbers in the hotel, electricians in the schoolhouse. They were good men, but she watched them like a hawk. She'd worked on enough projects to know that subcontractors weren't particularly concerned with the big picture. Their goal was to get the job done as fast as possible. She'd seen drywall men go in and put up a wall when they knew darn well that the electrical lines hadn't been placed and would have to be cut in later. It was her job to make sure that didn't happen in Shadow Gap, that one contractor didn't undermine another. Her time frame was too tight for foolish mistakes.

So far, she'd succeeded. There was only one aspect of the job she couldn't handle.

If Drew was going to continue coming to the site every day to work on the schoolhouse and generally keep an eye on the project, the least he could do was to act the part of the boss and be a little obnoxious. Why couldn't he carp and criticize and "suggest" as supervisors were supposed to do? Why did he have to stand around during his breaks looking so damned satisfied—and leaving her feeling so unsatisfied?

The South Dakota summer was heating up and every day, or so it seemed to Diana, Drew appeared in less clothing than he'd worn the day before. He took to wearing jogging shorts that should have looked ridiculous with the hard hat and goggles she required everybody on the site to wear. But hard, lean legs and a tight, lithe body looked good no matter what.

In the two months that he'd been there working alongside them, he'd gotten well acquainted with the crew and the subcontractors who came onto the site every day. His hard hat wore the words, Shadow Gap Police. Drew took the joke with a smile. But the culprit with the paintbrush, Danny Morris, a twenty-year-old

eager beaver, came to work one day to discover his hard
hat had suddenly sprouted the legend, Shadow Gap
Delinquent.

That was only one of many harmless pranks the crew
indulged in to ease the boredom and relieve the tension. Diana's hard hat proclaimed Here Comes The
Boss. Diana didn't care what Danny wrote on her hat
as long as he got his work done.

Every day she cajoled, placated, prayed. Every night
she pored over the project report sheet and checked off
the tasks done against their projected schedule. So far
she was running on time.

She lived, ate and slept Shadow Gap. The town became her life, her love, her obsession, inexplicably
bound with the man with sea-green eyes and sun-gilded
hair. When the project was over, she would remember
each day of it with crystal clarity.

As if it weren't enough to worry about her own love
life, she was concerned about Jeanine. Two weeks after
the launch party, Jeanine had gotten a letter from
Court. She hadn't shared the contents with Diana. And
there had been phone calls, too, calls that had brought
bright spots to Jeanine's cheeks.

One evening during the first week of August, when
all the workers had left the site but her, Diana stood in
the bank, gazing around with satisfaction. There was
no question about it, she was probably the only woman
in the world who got a rush from the smell of raw
wood.

It wasn't only the resiny smell she loved. She loved
the feeling of taking something old and giving it life and
value. In just two months, she'd turned Shadow Gap
from a ghost town into a promising tourist attraction.
There was painting to be done, of course, and the in-

terior work would proceed much more slowly than the exterior had. There'd been problems here and there. There was the day Dave had walked out on a scaffolding he'd thought was secured and found it tipping like a teeter-totter under him. He'd turned and scrambled back to the other end in time to save himself from falling, and with a speed that would have made Diana laugh if her heart hadn't been in her throat. All in all, she was proud of her crew and of the subcontractors she'd hired. They were a great bunch. For the most part. There was only one man who seemed to resent having a woman boss. His name was Harold Loring, and he was the subcontractor in charge of electrical. So far, she'd managed to avoid a confrontation with him. Perhaps, with a little luck, she could continue to keep the peace.

The next day, while she was inspecting the handiwork of one of her men on the bank cages, Jeanine rapped her knuckles on Diana's hard hat and said in a dry tone, "You're wanted."

"What for?"

"Clyde says Harold wants to modify the original plans. You'd better go see what's going on."

Swiping a perspiring palm down her thigh, Diana muttered an oath and slid her goggles up. She'd arranged for Clyde, who was a crusty old farmer and a man she would trust with her last dime, to act as a sort of unofficial liaison between her and Harold. "That's all I need today, to have to deal with Mr. Fixit. I don't think I'm up to it."

Jeanine's eyes flashed over Diana's face. "It's not like you to admit you're tired."

"I didn't say I was tired. I just said I wasn't up to a confrontation."

She got a clap on the shoulder and a sympathetic look from Jeanine. "It's hell being boss. But some of us were born to lead."

Diana made a face at her and then smiled.

When she stepped outside, Diana felt the South Dakota sunshine blazing down on her back with its familiar intensity. For the first time since she'd started the project, she wished the weather wasn't quite so relentlessly hot. While the dryness was great for their schedule and made it possible for them to proceed without a single lost day, the prairie was beginning to take on a parched look. There had been warnings issued to campers that no fires would be allowed in the forest.

Inside the schoolhouse, it was just as hot, and dark and dusty, as well.

"What is it, Clyde?"

Clyde, who was working to earn extra money to save his farm from the selling block, drawled, "Young man here doesn't want to take the time to run the electric cord down through the wall. Wants to run it up outside the wall through conduit."

"Where it can be seen? That's not what the prints call for."

Clyde shrugged, as if to say that was obvious to an idiot, but not to that particular idiot.

Harold stood watching Diana, his face friendly and open. He looked as if he wouldn't hurt a fly. But Diana had learned that under that easy smile was a will of iron.

Diana decided to play it light, at least for now. "So, what's the story here, Harold?"

Harold's smile widened. "There's no way in hell I can feed this electric wire—" he brandished it at her as if he needed to show her what it was "—up through that wall—" he pointed to the wall next to the door "—to that hole." Again his grimy finger stabbed in the general direction of the opening that had been cut for the wall switch.

Beside Diana, Clyde shifted his cud of gum from one side to the other and watched her carefully. Two other men, Harold's assistants, exchanged smiles. They'd obviously seen this routine done before on a male boss. Now they were wondering how she would handle it.

Diana decided it was time to stop playing games. "Are you telling me it's not possible for you, a man with your experience, to thread the wire through the wall?"

His smile lost a little of its luster. "No, I'm not saying I can't do it. I'm just saying it isn't worth me spending an hour fishing around with this thing when I could staple up conduit in five minutes."

"You're going to put electric wire in an obvious place on the wall in a nineteenth-century building? Don't you think that's a little . . . incongruous?"

He shrugged and smiled. "Won't be noticed under the paint."

With a lethal softness, she replied, "I'll notice it, Harold." Then she said smoothly, "I work for a lot less per hour than you do. I'll take the time to thread the wire through."

He reddened and looked as if he would have protested, but Diana turned to Clyde. "I'll need a plumb bob to drop through the top hole."

"Yes, ma'am." Clyde turned away, his mouth quirking.

Diana swung back to Harold. "I suppose you didn't think about feeding another line through from the top, catching the line from the bottom and threading it through."

He stared at her as if it were her fault that that solution hadn't occurred to him. "I don't do much wiring when the walls are already in place."

From beside her, Clyde handed her the plumb bob. Diana took it, her eyes averted. "Well, look at it this way, Harold. Every day we learn something new. Today's your day." Wrapping the bob on a thin strand of twine, she dropped it through the hole, making sure that the other end of the twine was still trailing from the top. Squatting down, using a pair of pliers, she located the bob and pulled it out from under the wall. With a few deft movements, she tied the twine around the electric wire, tucked the end of the wire under the board and threaded the twine and wire back up through the hole.

"There," she said, drawing the wire through with enough slack so that it wouldn't drop back and draping the end down the wall, her smile firmly in place. "You see, Harold? Nothing to it."

"The secret seems to be in knowing how."

That slow, honeyed voice made the nape of her neck tingle. Diana turned to discover Drew leaning against the door, his eyes alive with laughter.

They laughed again about the episode that evening over pizza. Occasionally Drew ate his meals with Jeanine and Diana at the trailer, talking easily with them about the events of the day. Then he would climb into his car and go home.

As she watched him go that evening, Jeanine said, "I keep thinking one of these days, he's gonna' ask me to leave so he can stay."

Diana shook her head. "I don't think so."

"Why not?"

"We're just friends; that's all." Lifting her hand to pull her dark hair off her nape, she turned to Jeanine. "Just like you and Court are friends."

"We talk on the phone occasionally, and usually in your presence."

"Well, Drew and I eat together occasionally, usually in your presence. And we see a movie together, usually in your presence."

"I would have been glad to stay home—"

"No one asked you to, did they? Drew obviously doesn't want to be alone with me. Now if you'll excuse me, I think I'll drag myself to bed." Diana let the trailer door slap behind her, hoping she was exhausted enough to forget how Drew had looked at her that afternoon. It had been the first time he'd given her reason to think he hadn't lost interest in her. Or was it simply her overactive imagination, combined with her wishful thinking, that had conjured up that gleam in his eyes and given her the swift, telepathic feeling that he was just . . . waiting?

IN THE DARK HEAT of the South Dakota night, Drew sprawled on the couch, his jeans undone, his chest and feet bare. An open book lay beside him. He stared at the opposite wall, seeing nothing. His work inside the schoolhouse was done. The paint was removed, and the old walls and floor hardly showed the scars. He'd taken the books to a bookbinder who'd promised authentic antique covers. How much longer could he stay in South Dakota and not look like a fool? How much longer could he go on telling himself he was merely staying a few more days until he felt satisfied that the vandals wouldn't return?

Satisfied. Ah, there was a thought. He thought of how satisfying it would be to take Diana somewhere cool and comfortable and spend several hours bringing her to the same unsatisfied state he was in. When he closed his eyes he seemed to see her the way she'd been tonight, tired but smiling in spite of her fatigue.

He wanted to kiss away that fatigue—and then put shadows of an entirely different kind beneath her eyes, the shadows a woman wore when she'd been loved well through a long, hot night.

Heat rose inside his body. He muttered a curse and picked up his book, only to toss it down again. He would get dressed and walk along the river. As he'd done the night before. And the night before that. And the night before that.

IN HER STEAMY TRAILER, on a ninety-degree night, Diana kicked the light sheet aside. She sat up, pulled on a robe and let herself out the door. Beyond the campground light, the woods, with its dark secrets, enclosed the clearing. An owl hooted, and the sound echoed eerily in the mountains. She wandered on, her lips curving as she remembered the tall tale Drew had told that evening after they'd finished their pizza. He'd been the consummate South Dakota native, trying to convince two Iowa women of the fierceness of the West. He'd started with the whopper about the echo that took exactly eight hours to rebound from Harney Peak, so that all a miner had to do was bawl, "Git up, you S.O.B." before he went to bed at night, and he had a ready-made alarm clock.

Drew had followed that with another just as bad. He'd told them with great soberness that there had been a creek in the Black Hills that ran so fast it boiled dry before it got to the valley. Even when they'd laughed, he'd assured them in a didactic tone that a man could catch a fish in the upper reaches and poach it as he walked downhill to camp.

He'd nearly gotten them on the petrified birds, though, mostly because there was just a modicum of truth in it. Diana and Jeanine both knew there actually was petrified wood in the Black Hills, so when he'd added the bit about the stony birds sitting on petrified limbs, the two women had almost, but not quite, believed him. Flushed with success, Drew had proclaimed soberly, but with a gleam in his eye, that when the birds sang, the notes left their mouths, turned to stone and fell to the ground, clinking in resonant dissonance through the mountain air.

Diana turned back into the darkness toward the trailer, her thoughts still on Drew. He was good company. She was glad he was there. Having him on site to share her workday made the load somehow lighter.

She liked him very much, as a person, as well as a man. He treated her with respect in front of her crew, and with a teasing deference in front of Jeanine. It was obvious he enjoyed her company. It was also obvious he had no intention of pursuing her. She wondered why he'd cooled toward her. He'd shown every evidence of being interested in her at the beginning of the project. Was he keeping things light because he didn't want to mix business with pleasure? Or had he, since he'd come to know her better, realized that Diana was a poor substitute for Jamie? The thought chilled her. Sighing, she reached the trailer and went back inside to lie down on her bed and stare into the darkness.

Was he lying in his bed tonight thinking of his cousin's wife? Was he that much of a fool? Diana's stomach tightened with a painful ache. Was this what it felt like to want someone you couldn't have?

It was a waste, a cruel waste. Drew was a man who deserved to be loved long and well by the right woman. Even if she, Diana, wasn't that woman, surely there was one in the world who was. And then she knew, with a sudden, stinging clarity, that she couldn't bear to think of another woman loving Drew long and well.

The heat didn't abate the next week. Temperatures hovered around the ninety-five-degree mark. Diana's emotional temperature was a close match, particularly when, on the next Friday afternoon, she stood with Drew inside the completed schoolhouse.

"You've done an excellent job refurbishing things here," she said, trailing a hand over the smooth top of one of the old-fashioned children's desks.

"So have you." He leaned against the wall and flicked the light switch. "The miracles of modern-day life. Without a power line showing."

She felt the distance between them as if it were an ocean. His work here was finished. He would soon be leaving. She turned to face him. "Thank you for taking care of the books."

"My pleasure." His eyes moved over her face while he smiled. Not a one of his thoughts was evident. He was pleasant, charming and thoroughly irritating.

Diana turned away from him and walked down the aisle between the children's desks toward the teacher's. She told herself she had a right to ask. After all, they were business associates. "Will you be leaving soon?"

He was silent. At the head of the room, she turned to face him again, leaning against the back of the broad teacher's desk for support.

"Anxious to get rid of me?"

She clasped her hands in front of her and looked down at them. "No, of course not. I just—" She lifted her head. "You've been a help, and I'll miss you. I was just wondering when I should start bracing myself to do that." She broke off and turned, telling herself she was several kinds of a fool. Why was it so impossible to lie to him?

He stared at her straight back, cursing himself for wanting her so badly that he read things into her words that weren't there. "You've been a help, and I'll miss you." Of course she'd miss him. They'd seen each other every day of the week for the past two months. She was being polite, speaking to him as a business associate and a friend. He'd damn well better remember that. "I'll book a flight back Saturday or Sunday, depending on when I can get the most convenient one. There's no rush." She turned, and he smiled at her. "Court's gotten along without me this long. He'll manage a few hours longer."

That beautiful, self-deprecating smile. How would she get along without it? "I will miss you, Drew." It was her last attempt to get some response from him. She was giving the man an engraved invitation. He didn't take it. He simply leaned against the door and said, "I know I'm leaving the town in good hands, Diana. The best."

It was a vote of confidence she would have killed for in the early days of the project. Now it seemed unimportant. "Thank you, Drew. That's very kind of you." Kind. Considerate. Respectful. He was all of those things. And oh, how it hurt. She tried flashing him a bright smile of her own. "Well, after that vote of confidence, I'd better do something to earn it and get back to work."

She shot him one last glance in the vain hope that his face would register something other than politeness. It didn't. She walked down the aisle and past him out the door, into the steamy heat of the afternoon, wishing she could go somewhere and immerse herself in a cool bath and forget how it felt to be so close to him, and so far away.

Drew stood in the empty schoolhouse, watching a mote of dust dance in a beam of sunshine. Inside his head, the echo of her bright, polite voice rang. Somehow, though he'd said all the right words, he'd gotten it all wrong.

The sense of inadequacy clung as he drove back to Hot Springs later that afternoon. By the time he let himself into the small apartment, his feelings of frustration and irritation had reached a zenith. He dragged his hand through his hair and wondered what he would do to make yet another evening pass. He could take a cooling shower, as he did every day when he came home. He could read the *South Dakota Sentinel* and grill himself a small steak, which he would eat off a steaming plate. Then he could watch TV, preferably something boring that would lull him to sleep. He could do all the things he'd been doing for the past two months to soothe his body and dull his mind.

But when he'd finished showering and eating, his body wasn't soothed and his mind wasn't dulled. He shoved away his empty plate and his half-full glass of beer. He wasn't in the mood to clean up the dishes. Nor was he in the mood to drink.

He'd told Diana he was leaving, but he hadn't really committed himself to it yet. He hadn't told Court he was coming back. And until he did that, the number of days he stayed in South Dakota was his own choice. Should he stay longer, hoping that, somehow, Diana would look at him and know she was seeing a man who didn't—couldn't—love another man's wife?

Long ago he'd stopped trying to justify himself to people. He'd learned, with his father as the teacher, that justification was a useless waste of time. People believed what they wanted to believe. He had preserved his integrity—and his sanity—by refusing to defend himself against any charges his father leveled against him. He'd spent most of his life achieving that control. He wasn't going to lose it now in a wasted effort to convince Diana she was wrong about him. She would have to find out the truth in her own way and her own time. Only then would they be able to explore the depth of the attraction between them.

How long would that take? They'd already spent two months together. What was the magic number of days it took for one person to see another honestly?

Maybe the lady isn't interested. Maybe she played you along, thinking that was the best way to get the bid.

No. Diana wasn't like that. He knew her well enough now to know she didn't have any of the feminine wiles he'd thought. If there was anything Diana Powell was, it was honest.

She was honest when she said she'd miss you. You've been a help. She'll miss you because you've been a help.

Dammit to hell. He was going crazy, staying here, waiting for her to see the truth. If he went back to Boston, maybe he'd be able to sleep at night. Seriously doubting it, Drew leaned over and reached for the phone to call Court.

When his boss answered, Drew was surprised by the lack of vitality in the other man's voice. "Things going well there?" Court asked.

"Yes. And with you?" The mockery in Drew's voice didn't register with Court. He seemed intent on problems of his own as he growled a pithy reply.

Drew smiled. He didn't need three guesses to know what was eating his boss. He'd caught a glimpse of the letters on Jeanine's desk in the trailer, the envelopes addressed in Court's barely legible scrawl. Court never wrote letters. He said that's what he hired his secretary to do. Obviously he'd changed his policy since meeting Jeanine. If Drew knew Court, and he did, those letters were part of a high-powered campaign. When Court wanted something—or someone—he didn't let anything stand in his way. If Jeanine had deliberately tried to pique his interest, she couldn't have chosen a better way. "Anything I can do?" Drew asked.

Court's "no" was rasped without his usual gloss.

After a small silence, Drew said, "I've decided to come back to Boston. I'll get a flight out tomorrow."

Court was silent for a moment. Then in a dry, knowing tone, he said, "Had enough, have you?"

Drew smiled wryly. "I'll give you a call when I get in."

"You do that."

He hung up the phone, sure he'd done the right thing. There were things he could do in Boston, work to be done. It was his job to think about new projects, and he should get to it.

The rap on the door was sharp, rhythmic. Unable to think who might be at his door at twenty minutes past seven, Drew rose from the couch to answer the summons.

Diana stood in the hallway looking like a schoolgirl who'd come to confess she hadn't done her homework. Her hair was still curling from her shower and pulled back with one of those long combs at the back of her head. She wore shorts and a matching yellow T-top that exposed the vulnerable hollow of her throat. She looked good enough to eat. And after all these weeks of seeing her, he was hungry. Very hungry. Was it possible she'd come tonight because she shared that hunger?

7

"WON'T YOU COME IN and sit down?" Drew said to Diana, gesturing at the lumpy sofa. "It isn't the Ritz, but it's the best the management's got to offer right at the moment."

His voice held a strained note, as if each word cost him. This was not the man she'd come to know, the careless, affable man who kept his emotions and thoughts carefully hidden behind a wonderful smile. This was a polite, controlled stranger.

What had sounded like a good idea as Diana played it over in her mind on the way home from work now seemed like insanity. Unable to think of anything that would allow her to retreat, she forced suddenly unwilling legs to carry her into the quiet, shadowed room. She and Drew hadn't been in an intimate situation like this since the night of the launch party. In all the long weeks of working together, they'd been surrounded by people and dust and noise. Now there was nothing between them but their thoughts and a yellow pool of light that shone on Drew's jeans and shadowed his face.

Without looking at him, Diana settled into the uncomfortable sofa. Had he eaten all of the meals there that he hadn't shared with her? It looked as if he had. One plate sat on the coffee table in front of her knees; the middle cushion was squashed where he'd sprawled. A glass half-full of beer sat beside a book lying open on its spine. He was using his credit card as a bookmark.

"You're very... alone here."

"I'm used to being alone." His lids dropped over his eyes. "What brings you out on this hot night? Although I must admit, you look quite... cool." Gazing at her was like tasting lemonade. The tartness and the sweetness were all there, satisfying, yet making him want more.

Drew took a chair at right angles to Diana and stretched out his long legs. His feet were bare, long toed, elegant. She told herself she was being ridiculous to admire his feet, and lifted her eyes—to his long, elegant body. He was in jeans, his blue cotton shirt hanging open and draped around his hips. The lamplight gleamed off his darkly golden chest hair and bronzed skin. He looked... vulnerable.

Why had she come, Drew wondered. And why was she sitting there looking as if she wished she hadn't? Obviously not for any personal reason. Thank God he hadn't jumped to conclusions and reached for her the way he'd wanted to when he'd found her outside his door.

Diana placed her purse carefully on the couch. "We've discovered something in the saloon that I'd like you to see."

Disappointment knifed through Drew. She'd come to talk about the project—and nothing else. He'd been a fool to hope otherwise, he supposed.

Almost while Diana watched, the old barriers went up. The charming smile lifted Drew's lips, and his green eyes fastened on her in a gaze so straight and direct that it sent her scurrying to put up her own barriers and stripped her of the energy she needed to see into his heart.

He said, "It's a hot night. You should have called."

"I know," she interjected quickly, not wanting to hear his protest added to her own misgivings. She rushed on with the excuse she'd carefully concocted on the way over. "I didn't call because I didn't know if you'd be coming back on the site before you left . . . and this is something you should see before you go."

"What is it?"

"I'd rather have you come take a look at it than be confused by my trying to explain it."

Drew looked relaxed, unmoved by her attempt to arouse his curiosity. "You're being very mysterious."

"When you see it, you'll understand. I . . . we can go in my car."

He told himself there was no harm in playing along with her. After all, he had nothing better to do. "All right. Give me a minute to get something on my feet, and I'll be right with you."

The darkness inside the car was just as intimate as his apartment had been. When he slid in beside her, Diana cleared her throat. By some miracle, she got the car started on the first try. But as they left the curving road out of Hot Springs and drove into the early evening darkness, her hands felt damp on the wheel. The quiet in the car was oppressive. In the pale golden sky, a thin slice of a moon hung suspended between daytime and night.

"I've driven over this road so many times, but never at this time of day. Everything looks . . . different, doesn't it?"

He didn't answer her. She didn't blame him. What answer did that silly question deserve?

Drew stared into the darkness, thinking that the gods must be laughing. He'd wanted Diana, and they'd sent her walking into his apartment. But he couldn't touch her. She'd come to see him on a business matter, and he had to treat her as she was obviously asking to be treated. The same way he had treated her for most of the summer. Most of this long, hot summer.

When they reached the canyon, Diana nodded to Ron, her security guard, drove through the gate and pulled up in front of the hotel, hoping the walk into the saloon would cool her heated cheeks. The trees whispered together, as if they knew the joke fate had played on her by making it necessary to bring Drew back to Shadow Gap in the purple light of the dying sun.

Inside the hotel, Diana turned on lights as she went, walking past the bar, heading toward the back of the saloon.

"Who put a hole through that wall?"

She wanted to smile. Drew was as possessive about these buildings as she was. "Clyde did after I asked him to. We only made a place large enough to crawl through at first. Then when we saw what was behind the wall, I told him to go ahead and cut a doorway." She ducked inside the opening, and he had no choice but to follow.

In the gloom, he wanted to reach out and touch her just to assure himself she was still there. He heard a small click, and the light of a battery lantern bloomed over Diana.

She held it higher, and light spilled over an old stage. The place was dusty, dark and haunted. Rough wood flooring that looked many years older than the rest of the saloon lay under their feet. A heavy velvet curtain that once might have been red hung in shreds from its rod.

She loved watching his face. He looked as if he were caught in the throes of ecstasy. She said, "They must have walled it off after the silver market dropped and the miners pulled out from the surrounding towns. I knew something was here because of the difference between the outside and inside measurements. You must have, too."

He took a step closer to her. "Court decided it was probably an old storage room and that we'd leave it closed up."

"Which brings us to the reason I brought you here. Knowing what it is, do you still want to leave it closed up?"

He wasn't looking at her. He was looking at the tattered shreds of velvet. "You know how much more interesting it would be to have an old stage in the saloon."

She took a breath. "Yes, I do. But I'm not the one who's paying for the work." She hesitated.

His eyes flickered over her. "What is it?"

Over the summer, he'd developed the knack of reading her rather well. He was certainly doing it now. "There's more. Upstairs." She nodded at the old-fashioned iron stairs curling upward.

They went up together, Diana leading the way. The stairs funnelled them into a small dressing room that was oven warm in the summer heat. A feather boa had been tossed carelessly over a rickety chair, a scarlet ribboned garter flung down on the seat.

Drew breathed in sharply. It was like taking that first, forbidden step into a time zone. "I toured Tombstone, Arizona," he said, "two years ago. They told of finding rooms below the stage in the Birdcage Theater, filled with beds where the stage girls plied their second...trade. I never expected to find anything like that here. Where does that door lead?"

Diana took a step back. "See for yourself."

Drew pulled open the door and found that he was in a bedroom of the hotel.

Diana followed him. A faint light streamed through the windows, illuminating the old purple wallpaper she'd already seen. This was the room she and Jeanine had used on the night of the party.

"Convenient," Drew murmured. "The girls did the show and then came upstairs to entertain privileged customers in private."

"It gives you a very vivid picture of the way things were done, doesn't it? Old buildings can talk, after all." She took a step toward the door and closed it, then stood back so that he could see. "From this side, it doesn't look like a door at all. It's papered to look like the rest of the wall." Her eyes met his. "Now you can see why I didn't want to tell you about it." She turned away, wishing she hadn't been quite so quick to face him. He'd buttoned his shirt, but in the heat he hadn't bothered to tuck it into his jeans, and the tails fell over his hips to brush his thighs. Even in the soft light, his hair glowed with a healthy sheen. He leaned back against the wall, his arms folded.

"Is that really why you brought me up here?"

She tilted her chin. "No. I came with you because I wanted to see the look in your eyes when you saw the stage, the stairs . . . and the feathers."

"Why? So you'd know how much extra money to ask for the renovation?"

She rounded on him. "No. My bringing you here had nothing to do with money or business or . . . anything like that."

"What did it have to do with?"

She was blazing mad, too angry to hold back the truth. "It had to do with liking the way you look when you're seeing something that pleases you. It had to do with wanting to see that muscle on the side of your jaw move when you're trying to hold back a smile. A genuine smile, not one of those dazzlers you flash at the world to hide what you're really feeling."

He didn't move a muscle. She felt as if her breath were coming too hard and too fast. After a long, long quiet, he said, "I like the way you look no matter what you're looking at."

"Drew—"

"Shh." Did he move, or did she? She didn't know. She only knew he was holding her, his mouth brushing her forehead.

At the wonderful feel of his hard body pressed to hers, the hot, demanding hunger poured through Diana in a flood. "Drew, please don't. Not if you intend to—" she paused, took a breath, pushed him away a little and lifted her eyes to his "—go back to your apartment alone tonight."

He stared down at her, his expression unreadable.

Her skin burned with heat. "I'm sorry if I've embarrassed you."

"You haven't embarrassed me...at least—" his smile had the charm of a rogue's and it was entirely too genuine "—not yet. We could go home and work on it, though, if you like."

Relief so dazzling that it almost overwhelmed her made her bury her head in his chest. He put a finger under her chin and tipped her face up to his. "You didn't think I'd say no, did you?"

"I didn't know what you were going to say. I never know what you're going to say."

His eyes moved slowly over her face, making her feel warm and caressed. "And yet I feel as if you know me better than anyone else in the world."

She shook her head. "You're a very hard man to know, Drew Lindstrom."

His eyes were alive with amusement—and desire. "But worth the effort?"

"Definitely worth the effort."

"Have I seen everything here that there is to see? You're not hiding any other secrets from me, are you?"

Smiling, dazed, she shook her head. "You know all my secrets now." And it was true. But suddenly it felt good. So good.

"Not quite . . . all."

The sizzling promise in those words still had her feeling shaken and dazed even after she'd driven back to Hot Springs with him and was climbing the steps of his apartment building, his hand on her elbow. Inside the lobby, he brushed at her dark locks. "Your pretty hair has dust in it. We'll have to do something about that."

As he led the way toward the elevator, she tried not to think of the intimacy his words implied. Though her heart hammered in her chest, there was a rightness about being with him that she'd never felt with anyone else. It was as if they'd been coming home together forever. Yet as they stepped out of the elevator into the hallway that led to his apartment, all the dazzling newness of knowing that Drew wanted to make love to her sparked inside her like lightning.

"I hope I'm interrupting something." Thad Lindstrom, bushy eyebrows and all, stood solid and unmoving in the middle of the hallway, a scowling rock of Gibraltar.

Even as Diana watched, Drew relaxed into a lazy stance, and his expression became bland. "Hello, Father. I assume you remember Diana."

"Hello, Mr. Lindstrom." Her fingers tightened around Drew's, and she turned a little, standing beside him to face Thad. "It's nice to see you again."

The bushy eyebrows dipped toward each other, as if he knew she was trying to soften his onslaught on his son. His laser gaze switched to Drew. "Well, can we go inside, or do we talk here in the hall?"

Drew opened the door and gestured for him to step inside. Thad strode into the apartment, stirring a breeze past Diana's nose.

"I'll say goodnight then, Drew."

Drew caught her wrist. "Don't let him send you away. He won't stay long. He never does."

"You want me to walk back into the lion's den with you?"

"Yes."

Their eyes met, a strangely foreign tenderness in his. "All right, I'll stay if you want me to."

"I want you to."

He lifted their joined hands and brushed the back of her knuckles over his mouth. "That for the tenderhearted lady who takes on lions."

A clattering sound came from his apartment. Thad had knocked Drew's supper plate off the table. Drew lifted an eyebrow. "The tenderhearted, *brave* lady who takes on lions." He smiled, and she smiled back. She couldn't help it. He said, "I'd better drag you in there before you change your mind."

Thad was enthroned where Diana had sat, the plate replaced on the table. When he saw Diana precede

Drew into the room, his frown deepened. "Decided to stay and see the fight, did you?"

"If you don't mind."

Thad grunted. He turned his hawklike gaze on Drew, then back to Diana. "What have you two been doing, rolling around in the dustbin?"

"That describes it accurately enough, I guess." With Diana holding tightly to his hand, Drew moved to the couch and sat down with her at his side.

"As usual, you refuse to do any explaining." Thad lowered his head and leveled the first salvo. "Do you have something going with her or not?"

Drew relaxed back into the couch, looking very Drewish, as calm and self-contained as if his father had asked him about the weather. His eyes flickered to Diana, and his mouth lifted in a rueful twist, asking her if she wasn't sorry she'd stayed. "You drove six hours to discuss my love life with me?"

"No." Thad wrestled around in the chair and cleared his throat. He looked like a man who had something disagreeable to say and wanted to get it out before it choked him. "I came to discuss mine. I want to get married. And if I wait until you're settled, I'll be too damn old to enjoy it."

In the silence that followed, Diana held her breath. Drew's hand was still closed loosely around hers. He hadn't moved a muscle, but she could feel him tensing. "I wondered why you were waiting."

"I was looking for a way—I wanted—dammit all— I thought if you ever fell in love with a woman and wanted her till your back teeth ached, you might understand how I feel about Ruth."

Ruth? Thad was in love with Blake's mother, Ruth? Diana stared at Thad, thinking the Lindstrom men had the infinite capacity to surprise.

"I've always known how you felt about her," Drew said in a cool, deadly tone. "I couldn't understand why you went ahead and married my mother. And neither could she."

Thad muttered a word under his breath. "So that's why you always aligned yourself with her."

Drew met his eyes. "If I hadn't, she would have been totally alone."

Thad thrust his hand through what remained of his hair. "You've resented me all these years."

"Under the circumstances, I think I've controlled my resentment reasonably well . . . all these years."

Thad sat up straighter, glaring at him. "Dammit, you've controlled everything too well over the years. Don't you feel anything, boy?"

Stop, Diana wanted to cry out. *Oh, please stop. Can't you see how you're hurting him?*

"I do bleed when I'm cut, Father." His tone was as dry as fine wine.

Diana's grip on Drew's hand tightened. Whatever she'd expected when she'd walked into the room, it hadn't been this complete exposure of two proud, masculine souls. And, she suspected, neither had Drew, or he would never have allowed her to stay.

Drew cursed himself for keeping Diana with him. Thad was the master of bad timing. There wouldn't be a family secret left under a single stone once Thad was done.

Thad grimaced. "I thought if I came here . . . if we talked, you might understand."

"I understand."

"And you don't mind?"

Drew smiled quietly. "You're asking my permission to marry Ruth?"

"Hell, no, I'm not asking your permission. I'm asking you not to cut yourself off from us completely. Ruth would never forgive me...."

"I see," Drew said in a cool tone. "You're here because Ruth sent you."

Thad made an exasperated sound, shook his head and glared impatiently at Drew, as if he were an obstinate child who could understand but wouldn't. "Ruth didn't send me. I came because I wanted to talk to you. I tried using the telephone, but that thing is an instrument of the devil. I called here every night last week. No answer. I called Boston, and some snippy secretary tells me you're still in South Dakota. I finally get hold of that boss of yours, and he tells me you're flying back in the morning."

Drew felt a flicker of sympathy for Marcia. His father must have made a real nuisance of himself to be put through to Court.

"I figured if I was ever going to track you down, I'd have to get off the phone and into my car." He lowered his head and scowled, looking for all the world like an annoyed bull. "I ... want to get this settled."

"And by 'getting this settled' you mean you want my assurance that I'll still come by the home place occasionally after you finally marry the woman you've loved for years."

"Dammit, don't go giving me a lot of fancy talk." Thad Lindstrom glared at his son. "Will you come to see us after we're married, or won't you?"

Drew thought of the years of neglect, the years of misunderstandings. He thought of the struggle it had been to come to terms with himself. He thought of the mother who had always begged him to be more tolerant and had told him in that soft voice, "He can't help loving Ruth anymore than I can help loving him." He thought of the woman who was sitting beside him, hardly breathing as she waited for his answer, who had taught him to "want a woman until his back teeth ached." And he knew that, on this night, with Diana at his side—generous, laughing, vulnerable Diana—it was time to put all the old resentments to rest.

"Actually—" Drew tightened his clasp on Diana's hand "—your marital status will have no bearing on my visits to the ranch. It's long past time that you and Ruth were married." He paused for a moment, and the quiet hummed in Diana's ears. "I wish you both every happiness."

She saw it all—the years of neglect by his father, the years of building the lazy, smiling facade, the years of pretending that it didn't matter that his father loved Ruth more than he did his wife, and Ruth's son more than he did his own. And now when the chips were down, Drew wiped away the bitterness as gracefully as he did everything else and proved himself a man worthy of any woman's love. In that moment, he had hers totally. And irrevocably.

Thad had the grace to look humbled. "I...thank you, son."

"When is the wedding to be?"

"Two weeks from tomorrow." Again the lowered head, as if Thad expected a blow. "We want you to come." He blinked, looked at Diana. "Both of you."

Drew's arm moved along the couch behind Diana's head, and his hand clasped her shoulder, warning her to stay silent. "Thank you for the invitation. I can't speak for Diana, but I'll be there."

Thad's shoulders sagged with relief. Diana could see that Drew's wish for happiness had meant something to him, but his promise to come to the wedding meant much more. Thad was a man who believed in action, not words.

Drew's father cast his suddenly shrewd eyes over Diana. His own problems solved, Thad had the energy to focus on her. "I did interrupt something here, didn't I?"

Drew's fingers tightened on her shoulder bone in another silent warning that confused her. She didn't know whether he wanted her to say yes or no. Which was the usual way Drew affected her.

"Has it occurred to you," he drawled, "that there are some things in the world that are none of your business?"

"Not if they concern me and mine," Thad shot back. "And whether you like it or not, son, you're part of that." He lurched to his feet, giving the coffee table another jar. "I'll expect to see you in two weeks." Another frown was tossed in Diana's direction. "Both of you. See that he comes, young lady. Watching a wedding take place might inspire this laggard son of mine to stop living this hellcat life he lives, never the same place two days in a row, and settle down with a good woman like you. Then I might get a grandson before I die."

Pragmatic to the end, Diana thought with helpless, silent laughter. Perhaps the father and son were more alike than they thought.

"Don't bother to get up. I'll close the door behind me." But at the door, Thad turned and looked at Drew. "Two weeks, son."

"I'll be there."

Harrumphing, Thad went out and closed the door behind him.

Diana wanted, ached to move closer to Drew. But she could feel him pulling away and putting up his guard. Deliberately, she leaned closer to his side. Just as deliberately, he let go of her hand. Chilled by the loss of his touch, she said softly, "Does he have any idea . . . any conception of the lovely wedding gift you've just given him?"

"If he did, he wouldn't admit it."

She raised her hand to touch him, to assure herself of his reality. He caught her fingers just before they smoothed down his cheek. "Lovely ladies who give sympathy so nicely should not linger in the lion's den."

"It's not the lion's den now."

"Isn't it?"

And it's not sympathy I feel. She ached to say the words.

He shifted away from her. "Shall I offer you tea to go with the sympathy? God, what a sight our dirty linen must be. You look as if you'd like to give me the world."

She dropped her eyes, knowing it was love he'd seen in them. Love that he didn't want. "Every family has its troubles."

As if he couldn't bear to be close to her, Drew sprawled in the corner of the couch, as far away as he could get.

"They were engaged to be married years ago. They had a stupid misunderstanding that Thad escalated by being so pigheaded stubborn." Drew smiled slightly. "As you see, he didn't learn from the experience. They had an argument. She married his brother, and he married another woman. Hence, me." An elegant, mocking hand gestured down his midsection. "And Blake. Blake is the rancher my father wanted me to be. Now Thad will have Ruth as his wife and Blake as his son. It's what he's always wanted."

Diana stretched out a hand toward him. She couldn't seem to stop wanting to touch him. "He cares for you. He just . . . doesn't show it very well. If he didn't care, he wouldn't have come here tonight."

"Sweet Diana. Always believing the best of the world."

Heartened by his words, she slid close to him and raised her face to his.

"Don't," he said, even as his arm came around her waist and he took her weight on his chest. "Don't give me your sympathy tonight, lovely lady. I don't want it."

She flushed. In her newly vulnerable state, she couldn't bear to have him look at her with such kindness—and such indifference. "You want me to go."

"I think it would be best."

The hurt deepened, becoming nearly unbearable. She turned her back to him, picked up her purse from the couch and rose. "Have a good trip back to Boston, Drew. I'll be waiting to hear from you about your decision on the stage."

He nodded, barely moving his head.

Knowing only that she had to get out before he saw how hurt she was, she threaded her way past the chair where Thad Lindstrom had been and walked out the door.

Drew sat staring after her. The rooms had seemed quiet and empty before, when she hadn't been in them. Now they seemed like a prison. She'd closed the door quietly, without a sign of temper. He hadn't wanted her quietness. He'd wanted her to pick up something, throw it at him, slam the door. It was what she would have done a month ago. He'd liked that about her—her freshness, her impulsiveness. Where had that wonderful spirit gone?

She didn't want to hurt you because she felt sorry for you.

He cursed his father, cursed himself. He felt as if he couldn't breathe. The apartment walls pressed in on him.

As he'd done every other night for a week, Drew shouldered his way out the door.

In the cool, early-summer night, he sauntered along the curving path of the river, his hands in his pockets. He walked past the old railway station where people had once come by train to "take the waters." The station was now a chamber of commerce building, dispensing maps to the tourists. He headed uphill toward the city hall. Built of buff sandstone, it towered over the town like a crown on a sovereign's head. Beside him, the river gurgled and sang.

Drew wasn't listening to the song. He was listening to his heart. His father was a triple fool. A fool for not knowing all those years ago how much he loved Ruth; a fool for letting his pride dictate to him; a fool for letting so many years go by. His father had acted as if he were going to live forever, as if life and love were things he could squander at will. But love was to be guarded and treasured.

The water gurgled; an ironic voice at the back of his mind whispered in rhythm with the rush of the river, *like father, like son.*

How was he any different than Thad? He'd stayed away from Diana because of his pride. He'd thought she'd see he wasn't the kind of man who would covet another man's wife. And so he'd let the misunderstanding build until it was too late to undo. He only knew he wanted—needed—the woman who didn't believe in him, the woman with dark glossy hair and blue eyes that could laugh at him one minute and promise heaven the next.

It was too late. He was going back to Boston. He—

Drew halted in his tracks, turned, gripped the railing. It wasn't too late. If there was anything his father had shown him tonight, it was that it was never too late. Time, so Einstein had said, was relative. There were things a man could do to speed it up or slow it down, put his hand on a hot stove, for example . . . or spend a night loving a woman.

8

TWO HOURS LATER, DIANA WAS tossing restlessly in her bed when the call came from Ron, the security guard. There was a problem in the hotel.

She clutched the phone, feeling hot, discouraged and highly annoyed. The last thing in the world she felt capable of dealing with at the moment was another problem in Shadow Gap. And the last thing in the world she wanted to do was get in her car and drive through the dark back to the site. But Ron was adamant. And what difference did it make? She hadn't been sleeping, anyway. Sighing, she pulled off her light sleep shirt and began to dress, casting an envious glance at the soundly sleeping Jeanine.

Deciding that a problem with the hotel was a fitting end to a miserable day, she pulled on her coveralls. Of all the buildings, the hotel was the closest to being done. The plumbing worked, and the central air conditioning had been installed and turned on.

At the site, Ron—the coward—stayed inside the shack and merely waved to her as she drove through the gate. Evidently the problem was exactly that—evident. Dreading what she would find in the old hotel, Diana stepped into the hallway and walked toward the swinging doors of the saloon, her nose assailed by the odors of new wood. Ron had left the wall sconces on, throwing a soft light over the mellowed old floor.

In the half-light, something moved. It was then that she saw the man sitting at the bar. Her breath caught in her throat. The sheen of his hair was unmistakable—and unforgettable. "What are you doing here?"

That smile. "Waiting for you."

From somewhere, she found the power of speech. "I . . . didn't expect to see you here."

"I don't suppose you did. But you did expect to see a problem."

"What is it?"

"It'll keep for another minute or two. Sit down." He gestured at the bar. "Let me buy you a drink."

She didn't know what Drew wanted. And he didn't seem ready to tell her. In the heavy, dark silence, she couldn't seem to breathe, while he appeared to be perfectly at ease. Had he come to say goodbye in a nice, polite, impersonal way, on the neutral ground of the site, to tell her in the subtlest way possible that he wanted her to forget what had happened between them? It certainly looked that way.

Her heart breaking into a thousand little pieces, she tried to match his detachment with her own bright, light, impersonal smile as she climbed onto a bar stool beside him.

"What would you like?" he asked.

There was something in his tone that brought her heart into her throat. No, surely, he hadn't put a double meaning into such innocent words. It was her imagination. Her overactive, needy imagination. She flashed him a hundred-kilowatt smile. "Sarsaparilla? As long as you don't tell my crew what a lily-livered drinker I am."

"Wild horses wouldn't drag it out of me, ma'am."

Sitting beside him, Diana caught a drift of expensive male scent. He wore lightweight gray trousers and a pale cotton dress shirt open at the throat, and it suddenly occurred to her that he was dressed to leave, possibly on a late-night flight.

He popped the tab of a soft-drink can and handed it to her. "Sarsaparilla, as ordered."

"Thanks. Put it on my bill."

"I'll do that."

Again there was that husky innuendo. Was she imagining it? There wasn't a clue to his state of mind. He looked relaxed, lazily as ease, just as he always did—certainly not in any hurry to go. Nervously she slid her fingers up and down the cool, moist side of the soft-drink can.

He swiveled his stool around slightly so that he could look at her. *Ah, sweet Diana. You're not quite as cool and unmoved as you'd like me to believe, are you? I'm a little frightened myself. I'm not sure I can live up to all your expectations. You expect bright, happy endings. I'm not sure there are such things. I only know I want you too much not to try.*

He said, "There's something I wanted to ask you," and then hesitated, wishing he were more sure of her. Still, she'd wanted to stay with him a few hours ago. But that was before he'd sent her away. How would she feel now? *Courage, Lindstrom. Have the courage your father didn't have.* "Will you go to the wedding with me?"

Diana closed her eyes and wished for control. She wanted to tell him no. She wanted to tell him to please, please go and stop torturing her this way. She should— must—tell him no. But the memory flashed through her mind of Drew talking to his father. She remembered that Drew had forgiven the man who'd allowed so many years of misunderstanding to go by before he'd made the effort to talk to his son. How could she repay such generosity of spirit with her own instinct to play it safe by refusing him? He might need her on that wedding day. "Yes, I'll go . . . if you want me to."

"I want you . . . to."

That was it. A simple affirmation that he did want her to go along and nothing else. No expression of gladness. Nothing. So. That was the end of it.

Too caught up in her own emotions to see the flash of intense feeling cross Drew's face, Diana swung her knees around to get off the stool, and bumped them into his. Physical contact with his lean thighs threw her into confusion. "Excuse me. I'm sorry. If that's all you wanted, I'd better be going—"

"It isn't all I wanted." He caught her elbow, holding her there on the stool. The old hotel creaked eerily, and Diana's heart thudded.

"I know I told you this the other day, but I wanted to tell you again what a great job I think you're doing with the town . . . and that I'm glad you're in charge."

She should have been pleased. But disappointment knifed sharply through her. The town was his first— and only—concern. "Thank you."

He paused. "Except . . . there seems to be a problem at the Oliver house." Startled, she flashed her blue eyes up to his. They were as enigmatic as the ocean.

Diana felt the urge to break into hysterical laughter. This had to be the ironic, fitting end to a disastrous day. After all these weeks of indulgence, he'd turned into the criticizing supervisor. "What kind of a problem?"

"I'd rather have you come and look at it than . . . have you misunderstand my trying to explain it."

The words echoed her own of earlier that evening, when she'd asked him to come with her to look at the old stage. But he spoke so matter-of-factly that she knew it was coincidence and nothing more. She felt weary suddenly, as if her energy reserves had been drained to the bottom. "All right."

In a state of subdued fatigue, Diana resigned herself to the inevitability of having Drew suddenly find something he didn't like in the town. She wondered if it was something she'd done or hadn't done and if the error was major enough to cost them more than a day or two of work. Diana followed Drew out of the hotel and into the darkness to climb the rise to the Oliver house. She fell a little behind him, as if by delaying the moment of stepping into the house, she could lessen the impact. He slowed his steps and caught her elbow, helping her over the rough ground, trundling her along with a speed and enthusiasm she resented, a character-istic, lithe swing to his stride. Did he have to be so darn eager to show her her mistake? Well, why shouldn't he be? Whatever was wrong in the Victorian house wasn't his problem, was it?

She didn't want to go with him through the cool, dark night, into that house where the old piano still sat with its silk-fringed shawl. He'd held her in his arms for the first time in that house, and how *much* she'd changed since that day, how deeply she'd fallen in love with a man who couldn't return her love. In a short while, he would leave her and she wouldn't see him again except for a few brief, perfunctory visits to Shadow Gap.

In the shadowed coolness, the living room of the Oliver house blazed with light from what seemed like a hundred candles. They were everywhere—on the ta-ble, on the piano, on the floor. When she'd lifted her startled gaze to his, he shrugged carelessly. "I knew you'd need light to see."

That shrug bothered her. That quick, careless lift of the shoulders contained more energy than Drew normally expended on body movement. "Where's the problem?"

His eyes flicked over her in a curious way. "Upstairs."

She didn't want to climb those stairs with him. "Can't you just tell me?"

A spark of unholy amusement turned his smile into the kind she liked, one of those rare, genuine ones he had in his repertoire. "I'd rather have you come and look at it than be confused by my trying to explain it."

The second echo of her words unnerved her. What was the man up to? His indolence had fallen away from him like a cloak. There was a restless energy about him that she could almost feel. What had him so energized? Curiosity made her turn, walk up the stairs and step into the bedroom.

Candlelight blazed from a hundred more candles— tall ones, fat ones, short ones—and the soft, flickering light-trapped rainbows inside the bubbles floating on top of the water that half-filled the old-fashioned hip bath in the middle of the room. Very slowly, very carefully, she turned. Drew stood with his shoulder against the door, his face smooth and maddeningly under control in the wavering candlelight.

"Is this the problem?"

A bit of his control slipped, he was tempted to grin. "No. The problem is, I promised to wash your pretty hair... and I haven't done it yet."

Nerves played a tap dance in her stomach. On shaky legs, she walked into the room and circled the tub. All she could do was play his silly game until she was sure she wasn't misreading him. "I can't see anything wrong with this bath. Other than the mystery of how it got here, of course, filled with water, complete with bubbles. And candles." Facing him from the other side of the tub, she lifted her nose and sniffed. "Magnolia?"

He shook his head. "Wild jasmine. The clerk in the store said it was guaranteed."

"To do what?"

His eyes laughed at her. "Whatever I want it to do."

"She must have enjoyed telling you that."

"Not as much as I enjoyed hearing it." He pushed himself away from the door frame and came toward her. His eyes never leaving hers, he reached for the strap of her coverall.

"Drew . . ."

Drew liked the breathy sound of his name on her lips. It did strange, wonderful things to his body. "Diana," he whispered, lightly mocking her, leaning forward to brush his mouth against her cheek.

His lips curling in a smile that was beautiful to see, he kissed her with the sweetest, gentlest of kisses. His mouth still fused with hers, he dragged her shoulder strap down. Every nerve in her abdomen sprang to life and tingled with anticipation.

She reached out to cling to him, needing him to acknowledge that he shared the hunger. He lifted his mouth from hers, but their eyes sought each other's as eagerly as their mouths had, blue ones searching green and finding everything she'd hoped to see there— laughter, understanding, desire. In a throaty voice she said, "Are you sure about this?"

He liked her all the more for her honest acceptance of the bath, the house and their need for each other. "Shouldn't that be my line?"

Shaking her head helplessly, she leaned toward him to rest her forehead on his. "Since when have we ever done anything conventionally?" His scent was sweet in her nose. Her other suspender drooped under the tutoring of his clever fingers, and her coveralls fell on the floor. She shivered slightly. Instantly he drew her into his arms and surrounded her with his warmth.

That simply, the decision was made. Diana had agreed to become his lover...knowingly accepting the danger of loving him. And now that she'd set her foot along the path of no return, she held him tightly, needing his warmth, his strength, his solidness. For the world had tipped eerily around her. She'd discovered that love wasn't something she could control and parcel out at will. She'd placed her heart in Drew's hands with no sure hope of receiving his in return.

He felt the throb of her heart, the thrust of her breasts through the thin cotton.

She grasped at one last, tiny straw. "What's Ron going to think?" There was helpless laughter lurking in her voice.

"He's going to think what I told him to think, that we're doing a detailed investigation of the house and I didn't know when we'd finish up." He lifted her chin with his thumb and buried his mouth at the base of her throat. "I didn't lie," he murmured against her skin. "There will be an investigation going on. But it will be of you."

Diana clutched his shoulders and arched backward, moaning under the onslaught of his words and his mouth. She had thought she wouldn't be able to accept

Drew's caresses without his telling her he loved her, but she was wrong. So wrong. He cradled her breast in one hand and mouthed it gently, wetting her T-shirt and the froth of underwear beneath, filling her with a pleasure that was nearly unbearable. He favored her other breast with equally loving attention until her nipples were peaked and heavy. Under the spell of his hands and mouth, she learned how it felt to be burned by icy fire.

She hadn't known she could want a man so acutely. "Drew..." She didn't know what she wanted him to do, but she seemed to have too many clothes on.

He understood. He knelt to unlace her boots and help her step out of her coveralls. When they dropped at her feet, she stood in front of him clad in nothing but the sweetest bits of lacy underwear he'd ever seen.

She lifted her chin to meet his gaze, allowing him to look his fill. She was going to undo him with her sweet, unselfish surrender. He clamped down on the urgency rising inside him. "If I'd known you were wearing these—" he ran a finger under the deeply cut peach lace of her bra "—under those—" he gestured to her denim coveralls lying in a heap on the floor "—I wouldn't have been able to get any work done at all."

"You thought of me a little?"

"More than a little. Much more than a little." He reached around her to unclasp her bra, his eyes never leaving hers. Her breasts were lovely in the candle-light, high, peaked, aroused. He knelt once again to slide the last bit of lace from her body to reveal her slender nakedness. She was beautiful, all-over beautiful, a sleek, satiny, beautiful woman. "If I don't get you in the bath instantly, you won't get there at all." His body throbbing with readiness, he lifted her and lowered her into the water. Every cell he possessed cried out in agony as he released her.

She floated from the hard strength of his arms into the tepid, silky water, which was exactly the right temperature to cool her heated body.

"Excuse me for a moment. Your bath servant needs to prepare himself."

He thought it would help his own hungry need to step away and undress. He was wrong. Bubbles floated just below her breasts, wetting her dark, rounded peaks but leaving them uncovered. Trying not to reveal his haste, he pulled his sweatshirt over his head and unzipped his jeans.

The sensual pleasure Diana felt from the water was nothing compared to the visual pleasure she found in watching Drew's lean body emerge from his clothing. He kicked off his shoes and socks and stepped out of his denims with the supreme male grace and the unself-consciousness that were so much a part of him. He didn't seem to know he was beautiful. Standing there in nothing but his cotton shorts, his desire for her evident, he most assuredly was.

He produced a large white bath towel, swathed his hips in it and twisted it into a knot. "Now I'm ready to serve milady."

Kneeling by the tub, he carried water to her shoulders and poured tiny streams over her that trickled between her breasts. She started with surprise and pleasure. "Relax, sweet. You're in good hands."

There was no doubt about that. His hands were far too good. He pushed her until she lay against the back of the tub, exposing more of her satiny skin. While she lounged there like an ancient Egyptian queen, he washed her face. Then his hands moved lower, over her neck, circling sensuously, until he reached her breasts. With deliberate careful attention, he soaped her with his hands, his fingers gliding in circular, repeated paths over her tingling flesh, a sculptor kneading a pliant subject with the satisfaction of an artist.

"I thought you were going to wash my hair."

"I lied." He claimed a glossy tip with his lean fingers, making her draw in her breath. When he followed the teasing touch of his hands with his mouth, she was filled with a stinging need that cried out to be appeased. Her body was empty, and only Drew could fill her. "I . . . please—" She reached out to him, her hands clutching his shoulders.

He drew away and looked into her eyes. "Yes," he said softly. "I know how you feel. You'd better lean forward and let me do your back, or I'll forget all my good intentions to take this slowly and make love to you here and now."

How smooth and sleek Diana's spine was, how supple her body. He'd never seen delicacy and strength combined in one woman the way it was in her. He took his time, enjoying the feel of her wet skin and her slim body under his water-slicked hands. He soaped and rinsed and then kissed her nape for good measure. When she shivered, he said, "You've been in too long. You're cold."

"No," she said, "not cold."

Drew gloried in her response to him. It wasn't sympathy that made her shudder under his touch. He gloried in her lack of guile. She was completely open and honest with him. He'd looked for that honesty in a woman for so long but he'd despaired of ever finding it.

Diana was drowning in sensation, drowning in him. She lifted her hand to touch his throat. A droplet of water clung to a tuft of golden chest hair. She trailed her fingers down his chest, finding and dampening the nipple nestled there, the nipple that was rapidly hardening under her caress.

He lifted an eyebrow. "My turn for punishment, is it?"

She smiled. "Oh, yes."

Drew put his head back, arching toward her, his body taut with pleasure. Watching him deliberately open himself to the sweet torment was somehow strangely humbling. The touch of her hands dampened his chest hair, turning it dark. "You . . . like that?"

He looked down and favored her with a wicked smile. "What do you think?"

She flushed, her blood rushing up to heat her cheeks. He bent to kiss her lightly. "Time for you to get out." He stood and pulled the towel off his waist. His eyes the color of an ocean storm, he held the soft white terry open for her.

When he pulled her into his arms, she was filled with mingled joy and need. She reveled in the heady, earthy possessiveness of his body pressed to her damp one. This was what completeness was. This was what joy was. . . .

The house moaned, a low, creaking, unearthly moan that sent a chill down her spine and made her wonder if she'd badly miscalculated; she'd examined the foundation of the house and pronounced it sound. "What was that?"

"I'm not sure." He held her close, comforting her, not tempting her.

Diana stood in his arms, surrounded by Drew's gentleness, his patience. The creaking of the house had momentarily unnerved her, brought her jarringly back to the present. "It couldn't be the wind. There's not enough wind in the valley today to make this house groan like that."

"Shh. Don't worry. Your Victorian treasure isn't going to collapse in a heap around us." He brushed a damp lock of hair away from her cheek, his mouth curving in a gentle smile. "You'd save it all, if you could, wouldn't you? You'd save all the life and love and happiness that's ever been in this house. A happiness pack rat."

She laughed. "I'm not that optimistic." As he stood holding her, she treasured this time before, this quivering deliciousness of being on the brink. There was a sweetness in knowing she would soon be his and he hers. And perhaps, oh, just perhaps with the loving would come love.

She was warm and fragrant from her bath, his lovely lady, and Drew didn't want Diana to worry about the house or the town, or the world. He wanted her relaxed and comfortable—until the time he chose to make her uncomfortable. Very uncomfortable, indeed.

A whisper of a breeze, the kind they usually got in Shadow Gap, made a branch scrape over a downstairs window. Diana shivered at the sound. Instantly Drew left her and went to the suitcase she saw tucked away in the corner. He produced two robes, both obviously his. The gray silk he gave to her, the white terry cloth he kept for himself.

Feeling a little self-conscious and knowing it was too late for that, she dropped the towel and wrapped herself in the robe. As she tied the tie, she lifted her head.

"Very elegant. Is this what the well-bred Bostonian is wearing at home this year?"

"I suppose so. And even those who aren't so well-bred."

"You're well-bred, Drew."

He smiled. "You can say that after meeting my father?" He shook his head. "The woman's lost her mind."

Gently he urged her down the stairs ahead of him, knowing this was what he'd wanted with her. Time to learn about each other, to learn from each other. Time to be together.

The house creaked again, moaning as if in pain. If he hadn't known better, he'd think the old house was deliberately trying to unnerve them.

Diana had to admit the creaking of the house was making her uneasy. She knew old buildings creaked and groaned, but this house had never sounded so noisy.

In the living room, Drew brought out the pillows he'd tucked behind the piano. He laid a small fire in the brick-lined fireplace and put a match to the kindling.

"You have checked the flue."

He smiled. "Actually, yes. And opened the damper."

He tossed her cushion onto the floor in front of the fire, put his close to it. "Will you sit down?"

Out of the kitchen came a picnic basket filled with crackers, cheese and fruit, then champagne cooling in a frosty bucket.

"You believe in being prepared." She pulled the edges of the robe over her breasts and draped the bottom half over her knees as she sat cross-legged. She was covered well enough, but she felt vulnerable, exposed.

He leaned down and brushed a kiss over her lips.

"Do you smell something?" she suddenly asked.

Muttering a curse, he straightened. A film of smoke roiled out from the top of the fireplace. "What the hell—"

The damper had dropped closed. Drew opened it. Before he could sit back down next to Diana, it closed again with a clang. He opened it again. It fell shut again. With a muttered curse, he pried it open and wedged the fireplace poker against it. Turning, he flashed a smile at Diana. "It's the small triumphs in life that count—" The damper slid closed with a bang.

The look on Drew's face brought a bubble of laughter to her lips.

His face a mixture of determination and exasperation, Drew opened the champagne and with deliberation, poured it over the fire. The smoke thickened, making Diana cough. Drew went to open a window, and the ragged shade slapped upward and thumped around the roller. He strained at the window handle, only to discover it had been painted shut about a thousand years ago.

With a muttered oath Diana couldn't quite decipher and was glad she couldn't, Drew pulled the door open and let the fresh night air into the house.

When the fire was out and the air had cleared, Drew gazed at the empty champagne bottle lying uselessly at his feet and said in a dry tone, "I should have known better than to try to make love with you in a damn *Victorian* house."

She looped her arms loosely around his neck, loving this handsome, annoyed, exasperated man. She supposed she should be sorry. She only knew that seeing him like this—frustrated, human, and very male— made her love him more. "We could go to your apartment." It took courage for her to suggest that. But she saw little need to be shy with him now.

"We could but we won't." He released her and took a step away. "I have an idea. Bring the cushions and let's go upstairs."

She started after him, and the floor creaked. He turned to her, his finger to his mouth. "Shh. Walk softy and carry a big cushion."

She grinned at him. His answering grin did strange things to her stomach.

Like teenagers sneaking in after curfew, they crept up the stairs, Drew leading. He headed down the hall to the room where they'd been before and gestured for her to follow him. Inside the room, he pulled down the tattered shade and closed the door. "Now," he said, and drew her down on the cushions with him.

Stretched out beside her, Drew took Diana in his arms and simply held her, warming her with his body, comforting her with his human presence. "If the house groans, we're going to ignore it. Agreed?"

"Agreed." The laughter he seemed to elicit so easily from her was deep inside her, like a chuckle that wouldn't come out.

He ran his hands lightly over her, rubbing the silk of the robe against heated skin. Suddenly the laughter was gone. She was lying down with Drew in a house that had gone suddenly quiet, and he was touching her body intimately. This was what she had wanted for weeks. And yet . . .

"Diana. Would you like me to stop?"

How sensitive he was to her every mood. How could she deny this man anything? She shook her head.

"What would you like me to do?"

Tell me you love me. She said, "Hold me. Kiss me. Help me . . . make it good for you."

He gathered her in his arms, his lips at her temple. He was smiling; she could feel it in the shape of his mouth, hear it in his voice. "Sweetheart, this isn't a contest. You don't have to worry about making it 'good' for me. All you have to do is be yourself."

Had she thought she loved him with all her heart before? At that moment she was filled with a fierce blaze of love and desire that she could hardly contain.

She gripped his shoulders, needing more than tenderness, more than gentleness. She brought him closer, showing him with her mouth and hands how much she needed his possession.

"Diana." Her response delighted him, swept away the thought that perhaps he'd taken advantage of her and should let her go. He couldn't let her go now. He needed her too much. And it seemed that she, by some miracle, needed him just as much. Watching her closely, looking for any sign that she was ill at ease and wasn't quite ready to let him uncover her body, he reached for the tie at her waist.

Diana felt those green eyes monitoring her every expression, while long, clever fingers parted the robe. She'd been naked with him before while he'd bathed her, but somehow it had been different then. They'd had water and laughter between them. Now there was nothing between them but warmth and heat and light.

Cool air touched her. Drew touched her, placing his palm flat on her abdomen in a gesture she knew was meant to comfort. Instead the weight of his hand on such an intimate place was wildly erotic.

Drew drank in the sight of her, wild silk in varying shades of cream, golden tan and rose. A flush bloomed at her throat; rosy nipples crowned smooth white flesh. Her flat abdomen with the jut of her rounded hip bones was pale, her legs tanned. At the apex of her thighs, curling dark hair nestled over her femininity.

He leaned over her, his mouth curved in a lazy, sensual smile. "How could you possibly be worried about making it good for me? Don't you know just looking at you nearly destroys me?"

She released the breath it seemed she'd been holding forever. Her breasts moved upward and, his eyes gleaming, Drew swooped and captured one in his mouth, savoring her as if she were a succulent candy drop. His hand explored, delved beneath the curls and discovered the treasure.

Diana writhed, caught on the delicious edge of anticipation. She clutched at his shoulders, the broad, masculine shoulders she'd wanted to touch a hundred times in the past long weeks. But his skin was covered with terry cloth. She wanted to feel his bare flesh, touch him as he was touching her. She reached out to pull the tie of his robe free, but he shook his head. "No. Not yet. There'll be time for me later. Relax, Diana. Relax and let me love you." His eyes caught hers, and for a breathless moment they were locked in visual combat.

At last she lay back on the cushion. She wanted, needed, to tell him she loved him. But she couldn't do that. So she did the next best thing. "Do you know what you are?"

"No, what am I? A chauvinist male who wants his own way with you?" he teased, mocking her affectionately.

"You are the most unselfish, undemanding man I've ever known."

His eyes gleamed suddenly in a way that rocked her heart. "You think so? Just wait a little. I'll show you how demanding I can be. But just now you're going to let me love you."

Before she could begin to think or worry or wonder if his words meant that he really loved her, he leaned over her and, using his mouth and tongue, explored her collarbone, her throat, her ear. When her skin was moist and blooming under his mouth, he raised his head and, with great care, fit his lips to hers, his hands coming up to hold her head and tangle in her hair.

He kissed her with tenderness, with hunger, with gentleness. His mouth gave her little surprises, warmth, a tender tug on her lower lip, a quick tangling of his tongue with hers and a teasing retreat. When she was breathless, he lifted his mouth and murmured against her lips, "You're all flushed and warm, sweetheart."

While her head reeled with the intimacy of his words, he claimed her mouth boldly, his hand tracing tenderly around the shell of her ear, his fingers gentle, his tongue inciting her to madness.

Her body pulsed, tingled, cried with need, and he knew it. Relentlessly he continued his sensual, loving onslaught, exploring her mouth, thrusting his tongue in a bold, sensual rhythm that claimed her as his. She clung to him fiercely, needing his physical possession. Her tongue answered his, and her hands pulled at the tie at his waist.

"Diana—"

She didn't, wouldn't listen. He was hers, and she claimed him, her fingers threading through the golden chest hair and circling his nipples till she felt the answering, hardening response in the flat nubs. She pulled at the terry cloth, wanting him free of it, wanting him only to be touched by her.

He humored her, lifting up to pull his arms and shoulders out of the robe. Then he lay back, naked, the white robe fanned out under his summer-tanned body. As he watched her look at him, a tiny smile quirked his lips. "Am I..do you like the way I look?"

She smiled back, knowing he was teasing her. "You're a beautiful man. Just looking at you nearly destroys me."

"Not beautiful," he said. At her echo of his words, passion and laughter blended in his voice. "Just . . . needy."

She reached out and touched his male shaft. He was warm satin, firm. When her fingers grew bolder and more possessive in their exploration, he breathed in sharply.

She went on caressing him, plying him with the warmth and strength of her fingers. He shook his head but said nothing to stop her, until she closed her fingers warmly around him. "Diana," he said in a warning tone.

"Would you—do you mind if I—" she stopped, unable to voice the words to ask him if he preferred the standard, male-dominant position.

"I believe this dance is ladies' choice," he murmured. "Just . . . give me a minute." He fumbled in the pocket of his robe with one hand, his eyes on her. "I want to protect you, beautiful lady."

She nodded, her throat full. How like him to be considerate enough to take responsibility for the safety of their lovemaking. When he'd finished, he guided her hips over him until she was straddling him. His eyes changed, darkened as she took him into her body and made them one.

His shoulders gleamed from perspiration, and his hair was bright with the sheen from the candlelight. He *was* the most beautiful man she had ever seen. And at this moment, he was hers.

"Don't . . . move. Just . . . give me a moment, sweetheart." He cupped her breasts, his eyes loving her.

"Take all the moments you like."

"You are so . . . exactly right for me. You know that, don't you?"

She didn't. She only knew *he* was exactly right for her. She leaned forward and threaded her fingers through his hair, her breasts crushed against his chest. "Am I . . . too heavy?"

He ran a hand down her back, over the curve of her buttocks. "A featherweight like you heavy? Not a chance."

She shifted a little, finding a more comfortable place for her knee.

"Ah, my sweet. Easy."

Experimentally she repeated the action.

"Merciless woman." She moved again, and discovered her pleasure increasing in direct proportion to his.

"Kiss me, sweetheart."

Dazed with sensual pleasure, she leaned over him, aware that his body was moving, demanding a rhythm from hers that she was more than willing to give. Her heart soaring, she gave him her mouth and felt his double possession take her with a fiery blaze past reason, past sanity, past thought. In moments, he joined her there in that bright world where nothing existed but the blaze of exquisite ecstasy.

She dozed on the cushion, caught in a dreamworld of euphoric color and light. A world that was slowly growing cold....

Drew knelt beside her and brushed a kiss over her lips. "Wake up, love." She opened her eyes. He was wearing the robe she'd taken off him only moments ago and covered her with hers. He passed a caressing hand over her forehead, pushing the hair back from her cheek. "You looked like a child sleeping there on the cushion. I didn't have the heart to wake you. Are you still tired?"

Diana resisted the urge to curl like a cat into his caressing hand. She felt languid, lazy, thoroughly loved. "Not really."

He was quiet, his eyes on hers. She wondered what he was thinking. Would she ever really know him well enough to read his moods as easily as he read hers? Did he feel the same way she did, his body warm from her loving? Or was he trying to come up with a graceful exit line that wouldn't hurt her feelings? The thought sobered her and brought her fully awake. "You want to leave."

"I was wondering if I could entice you to come back to my apartment with me if I promised you something to eat." He lifted a golden brow, and his mouth quirked. "As I remember, you're a woman whose heart can be reached through her stomach."

"How ungentlemanly of you to remember that." Relief coursed through her. He wanted to stay with her as much as she wanted to stay with him.

"A gentleman I'm not. I tend to be practical about things like food, and I admire women who are the same. I don't know about you, but I'm still . . . hungry."

Aware of his green eyes moving over her, their message of hunger having nothing to do with food, his face still darkly sensual and full of promise, she felt herself flushing. There was no way she could refuse him, no way she could deny she wanted the wonder of their lovemaking to happen again. "Yes, I'd like that."

They returned to his apartment, and after they'd fixed a light supper of omelet and cheese, which Diana insisted they eat on the sofa sitting next to each other in the spot where he'd eaten so many of his meals alone, Drew tossed a careless arm around her shoulders. Without looking at her, he said, "Would you like to stay the night with me?"

His expression was unreadable, but under his bland expression, she sensed his edge of tension. "I'd like that very much."

He took her into his bedroom, where he helped her out of her clothes. In the cool darkness, the ease they now felt with each other intensified their desire. He murmured words of praise to her, and she whispered his name in return. In the comfort of his old-fashioned double bed, they touched and explored, kissed and loved, bringing each other to the brink of euphoria again and again, until they breached the barrier and soared into the shattered brightness together.

When they were both sated with love and with each other, he pulled her into his arms to tuck her against his shoulder, in a deep, dreamless sleep, and she spent the night cuddled against his chest.

DIANA CAME OUT OF THE BATHROOM the next morning reasonably composed and ready to face the fact that he was, indeed, leaving, but she couldn't meet his eyes, and her cheeks felt warm. "Diana." He cupped his hand under her chin, tilting her face up to his. "Don't shut me out. Not now; not after you've so generously let me into your life."

Diana gave a little cry of relief and threw her arms around Drew's neck. "I thought you were shutting me out."

"Oh, no," he said with fervor. "I just feel like a damn fool, having to leave you like this. I want you to know that I—" he stopped, his eyes searching her face.

"What, Drew?"

Something in his expression changed. "We'll be together again soon, sweetheart. The wedding is in two weeks." He put a finger under her chin. "You did promise you'd go with me."

"That seems too far away."

He brought his mouth down on hers in a swift, fierce kiss, rewarding her for her honesty. "For me, too. It would be more convenient if you came to pick me up in Sioux Falls, but I don't want you to drive across the state in that clunker of yours. Maybe I'd better fly into Rapid City, rent a car and come pick you up. How does that sound?"

"It sounds fine."

"Good. That's what we'll do." He cast her a sober look. "You'd better see if that junk heap you call a car starts before I go, or you'll be stranded here."

She shook her head. "It'll be okay. Even if it doesn't start, you wouldn't have time to do anything. I can call Dave if I have any trouble. Have you taken care of everything here?" She turned to look at the apartment. It already looked bare. His suitcases were packed and standing by the door.

"I'll turn in the key to the apartment at the desk. Will you go out with me to the car?"

"Yes, of course," she said, wanting desperately to make time stop. He was hers, and she wanted to be with him. But what right did she have to feel that way? He'd said nothing to indicate he wanted more than a casual affair with her.

After they had walked out to their cars, he gave Diana a smooth, sweet possessive kiss. Then he climbed into his car. Her only consolation as she stood in the blazing morning sun and watched his gray rental car disappear was the thought that she would be seeing him in two weeks. But those two weeks of waiting would surely be the longest fourteen days of her life.

ON HIS FIRST MORNING back in the Boston office complex that housed the conglomerate of Bernice Foods, Drew strode into Courtney Hughes's office feeling vaguely disoriented. The rose-and-silver decor seemed foreign to him, as if he hadn't been in the office in years. But when Court turned in his swivel chair, scowled at Drew and growled, "Work going well?" Drew felt more at home. Things were, after all, the same.

"Yes," Drew answered.

Court's eyes gleamed with triumph. "Diana Powell is getting the job done, isn't she? Is it time for me to say I told you so?"

"If you like."

"Any progress made on finding out who the vandals are?"

Drew shook his head slowly. "I checked with the police again last week. They didn't have a thing."

Court sat silently, staring at him. "Are you sorry to be back?"

Drew met his eyes steadily. "My desk is piled high with work . . . as I'm sure you know." He paused. "I appreciate your giving me the extra time in Dakota."

"No problem. We've got too much invested in that town not to see it through."

Drew nodded, his thoughts going back to Shadow Gap. Even with the time change, Diana would already have been on site for an hour. By now, Clyde would have come to her with some complaint, and Dave would be ragging her to let him take his first break.

"Any progress made in other, shall we say, more personal directions?" Court broke into his thoughts.

"Your reason for asking?"

Court dropped his heavy lids over his eyes and avoided looking directly at Drew. Another all-time first. "I'm going to ask the spitfire to come out for the weekend. I wondered if you wanted Diana to come along."

Drew cast a speculative glance at his boss's dark head. Evidently Court's two-month campaign of phone calls and letters had finally had some effect on Jeanine.

Drew thought about what it would be like to go to the busy Boston airline terminal and watch Diana walk toward him. But did he want her to come to him that way, along with Court's current lady? Did he want her to be the one to step off the precipice, to come flying to him with no questions asked, no assurances given? She would do it; he was sure of that. His generous Diana wouldn't hesitate. "Not just . . . now. Another time, perhaps."

Court shrugged. "Suit yourself."

"Thanks for allowing me that pleasure." If Court heard the drawled irony in Drew's voice, he made no sign as Drew left his office.

After work that day, Drew inserted himself into the crowd enjoying the late-afternoon sunshine in Boston's public gardens and found a comfortable spot on a park bench. Two sneakered students from the huge student population chased each other around the suspension bridge; a woman sat by the water feeding the pigeons. The birds circled above her, squawking with greediness. A lady executive wearing a black business suit and pink sneakers dodged around an artist's easel. The world of Boston was busy, bustling, active.

He sat with one leg crossed over the other at the knee, feeling an odd mixture of contentment and frustration. For the first time in his life he felt as if he belonged, as if he were connected to the rest of the human race, and he was glad of it. But the lady who'd made him feel that way was several thousand miles away.

"Hi."

Drew was dragged back to reality by a young woman jogging in place in front of him. She wore the uniform of a college student, jeans, a sweatshirt and sneakers. Her smile was spontaneous, infectious, as if she enjoyed the humorous aspect of the world.

"Can you tell me what time it is?"

He shot up the cuff of his suit to look at his watch. "Five forty-five."

She rocked on the balls of her feet in front of him, blond, full of young energy, her eyes bright with challenge. "Are you waiting for someone?"

She was good. He hadn't sensed the come on until she'd got him talking to her. "Not right at the moment."

"Any chance of my buying you a drink?"

Drew smiled a slow, indulgent smile. "I'm afraid not."

"I was afraid not, too, but I thought it was worth a shot. You looked lonely and . . . thirsty." Her shoulders lifted. "Can't blame a girl for trying."

"Absolutely not. Better luck next time."

She turned to jog away and then turned back. "I only stopped because you had such a nice smile."

"I only refused because I already have a lady."

She grinned; he grinned back. Sketching him a wave, she jogged off.

The courage to ask. That's what he needed. He just had to make sure he was asking the right question.

ON FRIDAY EVENING Diana sat in the trailer watching Jeanine pack her suitcase. "Are you really sure you should be doing this?"

"No. Hand me that packet of hose, will you?"

"You're taking hose? You never wear hose. You never wear dresses. The only time I ever saw you in a dress was at the launch party. I didn't know you had legs until that night. They're darn nice legs, of course, even if they are a little pale from only receiving light filtered through blue jeans since you were four."

"Thanks." Jeanine thrust the pantyhose into the suitcase and snapped it shut. "We've been talking on the phone. He's written letters. I wrote back. I feel as if I know him now. It's hard to hold a mask in place when you're writing to someone almost every day. I've waited quite a while, making sure that I . . . He wants to see me again—" she raised her head, her cheeks flushed, her eyes bright "—and I want to see him."

"Okay. But just remember if you decide you want to leave five minutes after you get there, he's not going to send you home in a limo from Boston."

"I bought my own airline ticket. And the return is open."

"What more can I say?"

"*Bon voyage?*" She lifted the suitcase off the bunk and set it carefully on the floor. "Are you sure you're not jealous?"

"No, I'm not—" Diana's eyes met Jeanine's "—sure."

"Drew has called you."

Diana's eyes flickered away. "Yes, he's called. But he didn't ask me to come with you. I really can't, anyway. I should work."

Jeanine laughed and threw her arms around Diana. "That was exactly the right thing to say. I feel better already. I'll probably have a terrible time, but it will be better than working."

Diana said huskily, "Listen, you pessimist, you have a good time, you hear? If you don't, I'll come out and personally throw you in the Boston 'Hahboer' along with the tea."

9

WHEN JEANINE RETURNED from her weekend in Boston, she was glowing. Looking like a woman who'd seen Christmas-tree lights for the first time, she told Diana, "I paid my own way for everything, so I had him find things that were cheap or free. You'd be amazed at the things you can do in Boston for little or no money. You can ride the trolley all day for eleven dollars. The U.S.S. Constitution was free, and so was the Old North Church—although I did make a donation there in the little box they have in the back. They need the money for upkeep. You wouldn't believe the number of people who'd come to see that church. I bought him an ice-cream cone at Quincy Market."

Her color brightened. "And he bought me a hand-knit sweater from Greece. I didn't want him to, but he did it when my back was turned. He'd seen me admiring it. He gave it to me at the airport last night. I told him I didn't have room in my suitcase, and he said nobody else he knew would be able to wear it. He threatened to put me in it right there in the lobby if I didn't take it. Oh, Diana. It was like heaven. I . . . enjoy his company so much." Jeanine grinned. "He keeps looking at me as if I'm from outer space. He can't believe I don't care that he's rich, only that he's funny."

"Funny? Courtney Hughes is funny?"

"I know it sounds crazy. But he has a wonderful sense of humor. He laughs at the things I say, and I laugh at those dry things he says that make him sound so . . . overbearing. He says he's never had a woman laugh at him before. He's not entirely sure he likes it. He thinks he may be allergic to me and addicted to me at the same time, like some people are to chocolate."

"*Bon apétit*," Diana murmured, staring at her friend with an amazement she couldn't hide. Was this bubbly woman the same practical, wary lady she'd sent out of the trailer two days ago?

Jeanine's eyes dropped. "I'm to go to Boston again next weekend. He's sending his private jet for me. I—" her eyes flashed up to meet Diana's, a pleading look in them "—I may be giving you my notice, Diana."

Stunned, Diana stared back at her. "Isn't this awfully sudden?"

"Yes. That's why I'm not telling you anything definite yet. But he's pressing me to come to Boston and live. I told him I might consider it, but only if I found a job and an apartment of my own. I'm not moving in with him. At least . . . not yet." At the look on Diana's face, Jeanine held up her hand. "I know what you're thinking. It can't be anything I haven't said to myself a hundred times on the plane trip home. But I—I've just got to leave things open . . . on both ends. I've got to be free to go. And if I do go, I have to be able to support myself and have my own place in case things don't work out for us. He's agreed that my way is best. He says it's not the way he wants it, but he understands." Then, suddenly anxious, she added, "You won't have any trouble finding someone to replace me, do you think?"

"I won't have any trouble finding someone to do your work, but I'll never find anybody to replace you."

With a little cry, Jeanine moved to hug her.

Her eyes wet, she held Diana away. "Do you know what I was thinking all the way home? That if you had followed my advice and hadn't submitted a bid to do the work on Shadow Gap, I'd never have met Court."

"That's true, isn't it? So now you have to eat all those pessimistic words you said."

"I'd like them with catsup," declared Jeanine, laughing.

The hot, long week dragged on endlessly. And then suddenly it was over and Diana was packing her suitcase to go with Drew to Thad and Ruth's wedding.

Looking elegant in a dark gray suit, Drew, acting as usher, politely offered Diana his arm and turned to walk down the aisle with her like a courteous stranger, as if he hadn't just entered the church with her a moment ago.

The sanctuary where Thad and Ruth were to say their vows was done in the Gothic style of old dark wood, mellow with age. People sat in the curving pews, chattering to each other about their lives, their cattle, their children, secure in their world. Heads turned as Drew walked with her up the aisle. She was a new face among the familiar ones.

"I'm a friend of both the bride and the groom," she whispered to him.

"A very special friend. And we have a very special spot for you." He held her arm with infinite care and escorted her to the third pew from the front. "My aunt will be here soon, and she's promised to sit with you."

Drew was to be the best man as well as usher, and so Diana loosened her arm from his and slid into the pew alone. On the other side of the aisle, Blake, too, escorted guests in. Drew's cousin looked dark, sober and incredibly eye-catching, but it was Drew whom Diana followed with her eyes as he walked up and down the aisle, soberly offering his arm to the sweet-faced women of Rock Falls while their menfolk hovered behind.

Ruth had given Diana and Drew separate bedrooms at the ranch, but last night, during the prenuptial dinner, he'd raised his glass to her, the gleam in his eyes a promise.

Hours later she'd lain in bed waiting for him, listening to the rumble of male voices. Blake, Thad, and Drew had outlasted the women and were in the living room of the ranch house, talking and drinking.

When Drew finally came to her, the hour was late and she was warm and drowsy. Sitting at the side of the bed, he gathered her into his arms in the darkness and kissed her silently, his breath sweet with the taste of brandy. Playfully she drew a finger around his mouth. "Celebrating with your father, were you?"

"We tipped a few." He nuzzled her neck. "I was afraid you'd be asleep."

"I couldn't. I was waiting for you. It's been a long time since we've been together."

"Too long," he breathed. "Too damn long." With unerring accuracy in the darkness, he covered her breast with his palm, a murmur of satisfaction escaping his throat. "God in heaven—even my hands ache for you." She was wearing a satin nightgown cut like a slip with narrow straps and a V-shaped neckline. Easing her back to the pillow and stretching out beside her, he rotated his palm, rubbing the slick fabric against her nipple, his mouth nuzzling her throat, one knee possessively covering her thigh.

She laid a palm on his chest. "Drew. You still have your clothes on."

"The better to love you, my dear." He pursued her pleasure singlemindedly, his mouth following his hand on her breast, his warm palm covering her belly.

"Drew, I think . . . you're a little under the influence."

"Yes," he breathed, "I'm definitely under the influence. Of you. And God, it feels good."

He pushed her nightgown up on one hip, his fingers finding and tracing her hip bone. "Nice. You have elegant bones, like a good horse."

Laughter arced inside her like a bright rainbow. "Coming back to the ranch has gotten to you, Drew."

"No. You've gotten to me. Touch me, sweetheart."

She reached for the muscled breadth of his shoulders.

"Not . . . there. Touch me the way you did the other night."

"Your clothes, Drew."

Instantly, like an obedient child, he stood and nearly ripped the buttons off his shirt in his haste to pull it from his body. He tried to pull down his pants zipper and muttered a curse when he failed. Only after he'd applied his full, careful concentration to the task did he manage it.

Diana's naked lover slipped into bed beside her—and then over her, covering her body with his.

"Am I too heavy for you?"

"No," she whispered, his weight an erotic pleasure on her breasts, her belly, her thighs, "but I can't touch you."

"I . . . need you, Diana. All the time I was downstairs, I was thinking of this moment when I would be with you, when I'd slide inside you and feel your tight, warm body close around mine." Easily, for she was moist and ready for him, he made them one.

The heady joy of knowing he felt confident enough with her to do exactly as he pleased filled her with erotic pleasure. She adjusted her body to his, loving the feel of him, the warmth of him, the scent of him. How wonderful it was to be at this stage of loving with him, where she could thrust her hands into his hair and feel the touch of his lips at her throat and know that she was giving him exactly what he needed. How wonderful it was, too, to have moved so quickly beyond his inhibitions and her nervousness, with nothing left but the sweet honesty of making love in whatever way they wanted.

"I was lying here thinking how much I needed you," she told him, her hands threaded through his silken hair.

"I hope to God that's true. I can't get enough of you." He began to move, taking her with him to an even more soul-destroying height of erotic pleasure, sweetly at first and then with more intensity, deliberately moving to please her, his hand caressing her face, as if he were reading her expression with his fingertips.

"Nor I you," she whispered, unable to keep the shuddering sighs from escaping her lips when his thumb caught and dragged at her lower one. He bent his head and drank the sounds of erotic pleasure from her mouth, until at last he shuddered in final submission to the sensual pleasure she gave him, in as generous a measure as he'd given her.

Diana's thoughts returned to the present and her surroundings, a faint flush warming her cheeks. There in the church, the morning after the night she'd spent in such intimacy with him, she was unable to take her eyes off Drew. It gave her an acute pang of joy to see him bend his golden head to talk to an elderly woman, who was flushed with the pleasure of receiving attention from such a handsome young man and determined to make the most of her opportunity.

The names of people Drew hadn't seen in several years were starting to come back to him. He remembered Lillian Wigdahl well. She'd been his fifth-grade Sunday-school teacher. She hadn't changed much, except for those new wrinkles on her forehead.

"And is the charming girl sitting up there your lady friend, Drew?" Her eyes sparkled with teasing laughter.

"Yes, ma'am."

She gripped his arm tightly, and his smile faded. "You're not sorry about your father marrying Ruth, are you?"

"No, ma'am."

"You mustn't be, you know," she went on as if he hadn't answered. "Remember what the Bible says. Love is expandable."

"Yes, ma'am, I'll remember." Incredible how she made him feel like a small boy again. He remembered sitting in her class, feeling furious and rebellious. He'd been old enough and bright enough by the time he was ten to finally understand why his father had treated him with such indifference since the day he was born. He'd hated his father with all the fervor of his small-boy heart and he'd thought all that prattle about love was stupid. His father didn't love him or his mother. How long ago it all seemed. He felt sad for that small boy who hadn't had the maturity to understand that life is a capricious game, and sometimes the players get confused through no fault of their own.

The processional began. Drew followed Thad to the altar and turned with him to await the bride. Young Jenny's bouquet was trembling a little as she walked down the aisle alone and solemnly turned. Jamie wore a deep pink dress that brought out the red of her burnished hair and was full under her breasts to hide the bulge below her waist. Her face glowed with health and beauty as she walked sedately up the aisle. As Ruth followed on Blake's arm, the congregation rose.

Drew wasn't concentrating on the ceremony. He was thinking about Diana. Sitting there in her light blue dress with those silly, fluttering sleeves, she looked adorable. And he did adore her. He realized when Mrs. Wigdahl had asked if she was his lady, he'd been proud to say she was.

Blake's elbow poked sharply into his ribs. "The ring. He needs the ring."

While Drew fumbled in his pocket for the gold band, the congregation tittered. At rehearsal Jeff, the minister, had told him to put the ring on his finger so he'd have it, but the damn thing was too small. He hadn't been able to get it over the first knuckle of his little finger. He'd been afraid he'd lose it so he'd stuck it in his pocket.

Diana had never seen Drew look disconcerted. He was now. She was as relieved as everyone else when he drew the ring from his pocket and handed it to the minister. Why had he been so distracted? A thought occurred to her. She tried to push it away, but it wouldn't leave. Jamie stood at the altar looking gorgeous. Had he been thinking about her? No. That wasn't fair. He could have been thinking about any one of a million things....

Damn it, Drew thought. He'd better pay attention to what was going on. There was more to this being a best man than he'd thought.

The music was beginning. The wedding was over. His father leaned forward, took hold of Ruth as if he were afraid she would break, and gave her a chaste kiss on the mouth.

"After all the years you've made me wait," Drew heard Ruth murmur, "you're going to do better than that." Her hands came up to his face. She held him and kissed him long and soundly. When she let him go, her face was charmingly flushed, and she was laughing. So was everyone else in the church. Drew couldn't see his father's face, but the red crawling up from under his collar was a clear indication of his state of mind, and his whisper was loud enough for Drew to hear. "Woman, you're going to pay for that tonight."

"I certainly hope so," Ruth whispered back, and calmly turned to walk down the aisle on the arm of her husband.

Smiling, Drew offered his arm to Jamie. She was smiling, too, and as she took his arm, he looked down at her and thought she had never looked more beautiful. Was this the glow he'd heard women got when they were pregnant? He gazed at Jamie, and the thought struck him hard that he wanted to see Diana look like that. He wanted to see Diana wearing the serene inner satisfaction that Jamie wore like a lovely cloak. He wanted to see her body softened with the outline of a nestled child. Their child.

He wanted permanency. He wanted family, constancy, tradition. He wanted all the things he'd been running from for so long because he'd thought they were a cruel joke. Now he saw how very real they were and how much a part of life they were.

Diana raised her head to look at Drew as he came down the aisle. But his entire attention was focused on Jamie. He looked as if he were drinking in her presence with the avidity of a starving man.

Hurting with a pain that seemed old, deep and familiar, Diana forced her eyes away from the woman glowing with pregnancy and the man who held her arm as if she were precious glass.

Outside the church, under a brilliant South Dakota sun, Drew stood in the receiving line next to Ruth. Her mind in turmoil, Diana mingled in the gathering crowd, waiting for him.

Nothing had changed. He'd made love to her, but he didn't love her.

She closed her eyes and moved restlessly, taking a step back onto the grass. She had to stop thinking like that. She had to smile and nod and talk to the man next to her about how warm the weather was and how the cattle would suffer.

"I won't leave you alone at the reception." Drew came to rescue her, flashing a look of irritation at the man who'd usurped his place at her side. "You're to sit with me at the wedding-party table. Will you mind having people look at you and wonder about us? Diana?"

While she'd been thinking her desperate thoughts, he'd appeared at her elbow, looking faintly exasperated at being subjected to such formality and ritual.

"No, I won't mind. If that's what you want." She couldn't let him know. She couldn't let him see how transparent he was. She had to smile at him and pretend nothing had happened, that she hadn't seen the truth on his face a moment ago in that cool, shadowed church.

She'd looked lonely, suddenly, his lady, standing there in the summer breeze, her hair lifting from her neck. Drew realized then that he'd been thoughtless. This was his home, and he'd felt as if she belonged here and would feel as at-home as he did. He wanted her to feel at-home, to be a part of his life. No, that wasn't right. He wanted her to share all the parts of his life, the part of his life that was in South Dakota, where his family lived and where his roots were, and the part of his life he'd made for himself in Boston.

At the reception hall, sitting next to Drew, Diana wanted to believe, ached to believe in the small, loving brush of Drew's hand as he passed her the sandwich plate and the caress of his eyes as he fed her a bit of wedding cake. But she couldn't. He was acting out the part of a lover, and while one part of her soul whispered, *Forget and enjoy,* another part chanted, *It's all a mirage, and one day you'll wake up alone and lonely.*

It was ironic that, later, when Drew took her around and introduced her to people, she felt as if she'd dropped back in time. She might have been in her own small hometown in Iowa. The faces were the same, good honest faces. The concerns were the same, work, family, home. Basic things, the stuff of life. She understood these people. She was one of them. She would have fit in here well. But she would never have the chance.

"Well," said Thad, the flush still riding high on his cheekbones when Drew brought Diana around to him, "this is more like it. Looks like you two 'business acquaintances' are getting along just fine." He glared at

Diana from under his heavy brows. "Am I right about that?"

"You are," Drew said softly.

Thad started and leaned back slightly. "Well. A straight answer from you at last. Now I've got another reason to remember this day." He leveled a second narrowed look at Diana. "I'd like a grandchild sometime in this century."

Diana's flush matched Thad's. Drew slipped his hand under her elbow, giving her silent support. "You'll be the first to know, father."

When the reception guests began to kiss Ruth and Thad goodbye and leave, Drew caught Diana's hand and led her out to the car.

"I didn't tell Thad and Ruth goodbye."

"I did it for both of us." Inside the car, he drew her to him and kissed her, his mouth mobile, seeking her compliance. "That's for being so patient with all the family ritual." He sought her mouth again, taking it with an eager hungriness that promised possession. "And that's for being so beautiful." Once more he sought her mouth, taking it with breathless expertise. "And that's for me."

Later, at the ranch house, Drew went around turning on the lights, throwing glowing spots of brilliance on the soft mulberry-and-cream-and-heliotrope rag rug in the center of the room. With a mumbled word, he stripped off his tie, shrugged out of his jacket and drew her down beside him on the deep, soft cushions of the leather couch. She accepted the comfort of his body warmth. In the cooling hours of the evening, she felt chilled, bereft, and his warmth behind her back was like a balm on her soul. Maybe if she could turn off the switch in her mind that kept reminding her of the look on his face when he'd walked Jamie down the aisle, she could take the comfort his physical presence gave her. But she wanted more. She ached to touch him the way a lover would touch him. She ached to cherish his body, discover his secrets. She ached to explore the leanness of his thighs, the muscled solidness of his chest and the fine, gold hair sprinkled from his collarbone to his belly.

"Home after a hard day. Just like an old married couple." His hand settled casually on her thigh.

"Where are your Dad and Ruth going for a honeymoon?"

"California. Ruth's never been to Hollywood and she's always wanted to go." He grunted. "I'd like to see Thad on a Universal Studios tour. Or better yet in one of those impromptu movies they make, using the tourists as actors. Wouldn't my father make a great romantic lead?"

"I see him more as a character actor."

"Oh, he's a character all right."

"Everything is . . . all right between you two?"

"Don't push for miracles, blue eyes." He smoothed her hair back from her forehead. "Are you tired?"

"A little."

His warm mouth sought and found the soft hollow of her throat. "Too tired?" he asked softly.

"Drew, I—"

"I apologize for what my father said about wanting children."

Oh, please. Please don't destroy me with that wonderful mouth of yours while you tell me you don't want that kind of commitment with me. I don't think I can bear it. Not now. "You don't need to. He—he says what he thinks. You always know where you stand with him."

He smiled against her skin. "I've never thought of it that way." He brushed her sensitive flesh with a soft, sweet kiss. "He is right about one thing, though. I'm thirty-six years old. It's time I had a family." She tensed, and he lifted his head. "Are you surprised?"

She turned to face him. "For me, having children implies being married."

"I think I just asked you to marry me." He sounded amused.

Diana couldn't think, couldn't move. How could he look at Jamie as if he wanted to eat her alive and a few hours later propose marriage to her?

Her dress had tiny buttons holding the front and the back together over her shoulder. He unbuttoned one, and her dress fell forward, exposing a smooth, rounded shoulder.

"Please, Drew—"

"This day has been an eternity long. But if you're tired, we'll wait until tomorrow. We have plenty of time. Our whole lives."

She closed her eyes, the pain rising hot and deep inside. How determined he was to play the charade out to the end.

Drew saw that she was hurting. His own reaction surprised him. He felt as if he'd been hit in the stomach. He took hold of her and drew her onto his chest. "Tell me," he said.

"I want to believe," she said. "I'm trying desperately to believe, but I—"

"Believe what?" He didn't move, but she could feel his muscles tense.

"Myself," she whispered. "I'm trying to believe in myself. That I can take the part of you that you're willing to give and not be greedy for the rest."

He leaned over her, an arm on each side of the couch trapping her. "There is no part of me you can't have."

"Please, Drew. I haven't lied to you. You must be honest with me." Before she lost her courage, she looked straight into his sea-green eyes and said, "I saw how you were looking at Jamie."

His look of total blankness was not what she'd expected.

Looking at Jamie? He couldn't even remember looking at Jamie. He'd thought he'd made a damn fool of himself eating Diana with his eyes in front of all and sundry. Blake had told him he had. "Looking at Jamie? When?"

"When you were coming down the aisle together."

His blank look changed subtly, and though he tried to shield the blaze of emotion in his eyes, she saw it clearly. "You have a vivid imagination." He thrust his hand through his hair. "That fertile mind of yours is an advantage when you're doing historical renovation. But it's not an advantage now." He pulled back from her, his body relaxing, his mouth lifting in an indolent smile. He was looking at her the way he looked at his father. She hadn't realized how it would hurt to be closed out like that. "You're wrong," he said.

She shook her head. "I know you think I'm wrong but . . . I'm not."

His smile grew a shade more cynical. "There isn't anything I can do to prove how wrong you are, is there?"

She gazed at him, words clogging in her throat, thoughts tumbling in her brain.

"Stubborn, pigheaded woman." He said the words with a strange, aching fondness. "Once she gets an idea by the throat, she can't let it go." He gazed at her from eyes dark with frustration and a strangely tolerant amusement. She watched him warily. He sat in his usual relaxed posture, but she knew him well enough by now to know his mind was turning over at the speed of light.

There was a clatter and a bang, and the door opened noisily. "We're home!" Jamie's voice called from the porch.

Seeing Drew and Diana sitting on the couch—Diana's face flushed, Drew's cool—Jamie looked disconcerted. Blake followed her in, his arms full of wedding gifts. "Aren't they here? They should be. Their car's here." He cast a quick glance over the two on the couch, took in the expressions on their faces and closed his mouth and the door. In a dry low tone, he said to Drew, "I'm sorry we aren't interrupting anything." He laid the gift-wrapped boxes on the hall table.

Elaborately casual, Jamie turned her back to them and needlessly stacked one package on top of the other. "You'll have a snack with us, won't you?"

"I don't think either of us is very hungry, pet," Drew said easily. "You and Blake go ahead."

"Well, come out in the kitchen and sit with us while we eat."

"Diana and I have something we need to discuss in private."

"It can wait," Diana said quickly, her eyes avoiding Drew's. She jumped to her feet. "Can I help you in the kitchen?"

Jamie cast an anxious glance at Diana's face. "Yes, if you like."

Inside the brightly lit kitchen, Jamie indicated the stool where Diana could sit while she poured water in the coffee maker. Her smile bright, her hands quick, she began the preparations for the light meal. "Our daughter Jenny is staying over with a girlfriend tonight, Polly Edmonds. Perhaps you saw her with Jenny at the reception. They're great friends. Jenny's very lucky to find a bosom buddy like Polly. Young girls need someone to confide in."

When Jamie finished making the coffee, she turned, folded her arms and leaned back against the counter. "And maybe young women need a confidant, too." She smiled at Diana. "Would it be all right if I buttoned up your dress? In my condition, I don't want my husband exposed to anymore attractive female flesh than he can see on television." Her smile was gentle.

Hastily Diana's hands went to her dress. "You look lovely. Your husband has no reason to look anywhere but at you." The button eluded her grasp.

Jamie came close to Diana and caught the edges of the blue dress to slip the button through. When she finished, she stepped back. "We expected to be interrupting something when we came in. We didn't think we'd find two people sitting on the couch looking as if they'd like to kill each other." Jamie put a gentle finger under Diana's chin. "He loves you. I could see it in his eyes today every time he looked at you. I knew he was waiting for the time he could be alone with you."

"You're mistaken."

"I don't think so. I've had a few years of experience learning to decode the repertoire of Lindstrom expressions. There's this one that reminds me of a cat that's got somebody standing on its tail—" Jamie brought her eyebrows down and looked like a genuine version of Thad "—and it means a cow kicked me and get out the liniment or get out of the room. And there's this one—" Jamie smiled, but the smile was dark with threat, "that tells me the price of cattle dropped six cents per pound today and I could sure use a kiss. Then there's this one—" she smoothed her face and looked so much like Drew it was uncanny "—that tells me the emotions the man is feeling are so deep he doesn't even want to think about them. The trouble is, sometimes I get them confused and I hand out liniment when I should be handing out kisses or vice versa. The vice versa is especially bad."

Diana smiled. She could see why the Lindstrom men loved Jamie. She was beginning to love her, too.

"Don't give up, Diana. He's a keeper. Do you know what a keeper is?"

"A fish that's big enough to keep. The little ones you throw back."

Jamie's eyes danced. "Exactly. I think the coffee will be ready in a minute. Would you like to go comb your hair and wash your hands before I call the men in?"

"CAN I OFFER YOU some of your brandy?"

Drew gave Blake a sardonic look. "You're the soul of hospitality."

"Well, think of it this way. You haven't lost a cousin, you've gained a brother." His mouth quirking with amusement, Blake handed the brandy snifter to Drew and eased down on the couch beside him.

"You've always been my brother. The one I couldn't keep up with."

Blake trailed his eyes down over Drew's expensive silk shirt, striped tie and Moroccan leather shoes. "I'd say you've done well enough, cousin."

Drew gave the snifter a turn, got restlessly to his feet and walked to the mantel. "What the hell difference does it make?"

"'What the hell difference does it make?'" Blake echoed. "As I remember, it made a great deal of difference to you. What you did, who you were, used to be very important to you."

"Did it?"

"You wanted to win every fight, as I recall. You also wanted to win every woman. What was it they called you? The Rake of Rock Falls?"

Drew scowled at his cousin. "I've never won any fights with you."

"And now you no longer give a damn about your image, and you're eating your heart out for one woman." Blake lifted the glass to him. "Congratulations to my new brother. You've grown up. Better late than never. Now that you've got that chip off your shoulder, you and I can be the friends we were meant to be."

"We kissed and made up once before," Drew drawled. "Isn't that enough?"

Blake sipped the brandy, savoring it, swallowing it slowly. "Evidently not. Come on, Drew, I'm trying to ease into giving you some good, brotherly advice."

"Why don't you just spit it out and forget the easing?"

Blake smiled. "That sounds like Thad. Okay, here it is. If you want a woman, go after her."

"With that advice and a quarter, I can make a phone call."

"It didn't look like things were going so well there on the couch. She's a damn fine woman from what I've seen of her and—"

"I don't need you to tell me that."

"Dammit, Drew, I—You never make it easy for me, do you? Look, you're a success. You went after what you wanted and you got it. I'm just saying you can do the same thing in your personal life." He paused, frowned. "It took me a long time to figure out that a man has a right to go after the woman he wants. I just thought I'd save you some time."

Drew set the brandy glass down on the mantel. "She thinks I'm in love with your wife."

Blake snorted. "Any fool can see that's not true. Any fool, that is, except the one who's in love with you."

Drew lifted his head, his eyes blazing. He grasped Blake's arm. "If I could be sure that was true—"

Blake smiled, a sleek, self-assured smile. "If it isn't, I'll buy you another fancy silk shirt just like the one you're wearing."

The swinging doors opened, and Jamie called them into the kitchen to have a sandwich and some coffee.

Drew sat opposite Diana, willing her to meet his eyes. She was looking anywhere but at him. Jamie had taken up the burden of the conversation, talking to Diana about her work at school. Diana shared some of her experiences about Shadow Gap, her face coloring when she spoke of the Victorian house that had belonged to the banker Oliver. Drew sat there watching her, aching, the tension in him building to an intolerable peak. During the first lull in the conversation, he said to Diana, "Are you through with your coffee?"

"Yes, I guess so—"

In one lightning move, he scooped her up off the chair. Holding her in his arms, he turned to Blake. "We're going to bed."

His lips quirking, Blake nodded his dark head. "And I thought you couldn't move fast, cousin. How wrong I was. I'm sure you're...fatigued and need a long night's rest. Pleasant dreams."

Those words earned him a chiding look from his wife.

Diana saw her chance to escape from a momentarily distracted Drew and kicked her feet impatiently. "Drew, put me down." She should have known better than to try. He had the look on his face that Jamie had said a cat got when someone stepped on its tail.

"No." He swung around and hauled her up the stairs with more force than grace and carried her into his bedroom, kicking the door shut behind him. He placed her on the bed, loosening his grip on her arms, giving her freedom. Her eyes riveted to his, she didn't move. He trailed a hand down her throat and laid it gently over her breast. A soft gasp of pleasure escaped her lips.

"Even thinking I love another woman you can't stop responding to me, can you, my generous lady?"

"Drew, please, don't—don't destroy what we had—"

"I don't intend to destroy what we had. I intend to build on what we have."

"You don't love me—"

"I don't believe in love. But I believe in you, even if you don't believe in me."

"I believe in you, it's just that—" She stopped, stricken, unable to go on. He'd never looked at her like that before, as if she were a stranger he didn't understand.

He leaned over her, and his mouth and hands turned relentless, trailing teasing caresses over her face. "Don't stop, sweet. You've never lied to me or held anything back before. Don't start now."

When she said nothing, he braced himself, his hands on each side of her body, and raised himself up to look at her. "Tell me, Diana. What did I do to make you think I'm still in love with Jamie?"

She felt as if she'd made a terrible mistake she could never undo. Yet she'd seen his face in the church and she'd known the truth and felt . . . betrayed. Nevertheless, he was entitled to an explanation. "I saw you looking at her as you were coming down the aisle and I knew what you were thinking."

"What was I thinking?" He leaned over and applied himself to the delicate task of tasting the skin at the base of her throat.

Her voice low, husky, she said, "You were thinking that . . . you wanted her." She gasped with pleasure at the onslaught of his mouth, her hands going instinctively to his chest, her fingers raking through his chest hair, her palms teasing his nipples.

"I wanted her. I'm your lover, but I wanted her." His words were dark, ironic, mocking. "Do you really think I'm capable of that hypocrisy?"

"It isn't hypocrisy to want someone you love," she cried.

"Do you want me? And do you love me?" In the silence, she stared up at him. "An honest answer, Diana."

"Yes," she whispered, "and yes."

He smiled, quite satisfied. "Thank you for that, at least. You're a wonderful lover, sweet, but when it comes to reading minds and coming to logical conclusions, you're a colossal failure. I may have been looking at Jamie, but I was thinking about you and how much I want to see you carrying our child."

"That can't be true."

"Are you calling me a liar?"

Looking at the slant of his mouth, she wouldn't have dreamed of it.

Slowly, carefully, he unbuttoned the top of her dress. "I cared for her once, yes. But she's my cousin's wife now. When I look at her, I see the sister I never had. But you—what I feel for you isn't a lie. I don't know about romantic, hearts-and-flowers, bells-ringing and sky-falling love. I don't know if it even exists. All I know is that I want you and need you. And I seem to go on wanting you and needing you no matter how far apart we are . . . or how close we are. You've given me a thirst for you that I can't slake." Her dress fell to her waist, and her smooth breasts were bared to his mouth. He tasted each one slowly, lovingly until her breathing altered and her body warmed with desire.

"Drew, you're not playing fair—"

"No, sweetheart, I'm not playing fair, I'm playing for keeps. We've long since gone past the point of fairness." He lifted her dress away from her body and then, with infinite care, divested her of the rest of her clothes. When he stood to strip out of his own, his eyes locked with hers. "Do you believe me?"

Warm and naked, he sat down on the bed beside her and gripped her shoulders. "Do you, Diana?"

"I want to. Very badly. But I—"

He should let her go. He should get up and walk away from her. For years he'd refused to prove himself to his father, to other women, to Blake and even to Jamie. He'd humbled himself to no one. He'd lived his life the way he believed it should be lived, and he hadn't given a damn about anybody else. But as he looked down and saw, not the beauty of her body but the vulnerability in her face, he knew he couldn't turn his back on her, not this time. For this woman, the one woman who had the courage to lie there unmoving, wearing nothing but love in her eyes, he would stay and finally try to make her see the truth.

"What is love, Diana? Is this love?" He kissed her lightly on the mouth. "Is it love that makes me ache to touch you like this?" He grazed her breast with a butterfly brush of his fingertips. "Is it love that makes me feel better when I see you walk into a room? Is it love that tells me I'd be happy spending the rest of my life with you and watching you grow round with our child?" He rubbed her warm belly, sending shock waves of a deeper warmth coursing through her.

"I don't know, Drew. I don't know what love is. I only know that I want all of yours."

"How do you know that you don't have it? I know, as sure as the sun will rise in the morning, that I will never leave you, or cheat on you with another woman." His slow rubbing circled lower, the heel of his hand brushing the dark curls above her femininity. "Is that love?"

"Drew..." The low, husky tone of his voice and his words were destroying her.

"Decide, Diana. Tell me what love is."

"Love is what I feel for you—"

"But you think sex is what I feel for you?"

"Drew, please..." That slow, relentless circling was driving her wild.

"Tell me, Diana. And when you decide... tell me what you want me to do. Do you want me to go... or stay and love you in the only way I know how?"

For a long, breathless moment, she gazed at him, at his slightly mussed blond hair, his tanned, glorious body and his eyes that were dark with desire for her. He wanted her to love him, live with him and have his children. What more could she possibly ask of him? Her heart brimming with emotion, she reached for him.

"Is this love, Diana—the way you make me feel, the way I can make you feel when we're together like this?" She shook her head helplessly, caught in the throes of the mindless pleasure he gave her so effortlessly. He leaned over her and kissed her, his mouth full, sensuous, demanding. "Is it, sweetheart? Could I love you like this if I wanted another woman?"

"No," she whispered. "No."

"Are you sure?"

"Yes. Yes."

He gave a low, deep groan of satisfaction and with the same inexorable gentleness of his caresses, he joined her body with his and loved her, and she him, until they climbed the heights and then murmured love words to each other and fell asleep, tangled together like children.

10

As WORK WEEKS WENT, it fell on the scale halfway between bad and disastrous. Clyde had been out sick for three days. A bolt had broken on the bucket of the dozer and the paint suppliers had sent Sizzling Magenta instead of Colonial Blue. One of the men working on the Fargo building had caught his elbow on a protruding nail. It had been a minor cut, one Diana had swabbed with antiseptic and bandaged with gauze from the first-aid kit, but it had shaken her. Worst of all she missed Drew. She missed seeing him come out of the schoolhouse wearing a smeared coat of green paint at hip level on his shorts, and she missed his teasing comments and his maddening smile. She'd caught herself watching for him, even though she knew he was miles away in Boston. And what was worse, last night he'd called to say he wouldn't make it to South Dakota that weekend. By Friday night, when Diana watched Jeanine climb into Court's company jet and fly off for another weekend in the city, Diana felt as if nothing would go right again.

The next morning, on Saturday, her breakfast egg was rubbery and the Laundromat was full of fanatically clean tourists washing the dirty clothing they'd purposely stuffed in their suitcases before they'd left home. The car didn't want to make the trip to Shadow Gap. Diana finally shepherded Sam through the gate a few minutes later, only to find the town site deserted and a note in Ron's van instead of Ron.

Lady down the road a piece in trouble with a flat tire. Knew you would be here soon so went with her to help fix it. Be back as soon as I can.

Ron

When Diana broke for lunch a few hours later and stepped into the hotel, Ron still hadn't returned and the wind was in an odd direction and coming through the canyon like an express train, whistling noisily around the buildings. Telling herself it was the rattle of the wind that made her dislike being alone in the old town, Diana climbed up on the bar stool and unwrapped her sandwich.

While she munched, she pondered the mystery of Ron's continuing absence. Should she go looking for him? If she did, it would mean leaving Shadow Gap entirely unguarded. Was it possible he was in trouble? Not likely. Ron was a six-foot-four, two-hundred-and-twenty-pound football linebacker. If anybody was in trouble, it wouldn't be Ron.

A shiver coursed up her spine. She'd never been in Shadow Gap alone before, and that darned prairie wind was whining very oddly.

Then she heard them. The regular creaks. One after another. In rhythm. Like someone walking in the rooms above her.

She laid her sandwich down carefully so it wouldn't make any noise. She didn't want whoever was upstairs to hear her lettuce crunching. No, there couldn't really be anybody upstairs. It was the wind and her imagination....

The creaks began again, nice and even. The back of her neck prickled. He wasn't being careful or particularly quiet. Was it possible he didn't know she was down there? On the other hand, how could he? He wouldn't have heard her come in.

Her breath stopped in her throat. The sensible, sane thing to do was to get out of there and run like crazy.

Then what? Leave him to do whatever damage he was doing up there?

Maybe it wasn't somebody looking to do damage. Maybe it was a clean-clothed tourist looking for a free room for the night.

What kind of crazy fool would come into a construction site when there were a dozen signs warning him to stay out?

A crazy fool who wasn't looking for accommodation. A crazy fool with trouble on the brain. A crazy fool who knew where to find the winding stair and the escape door behind the stage because he'd seen a set of blueprints—and had a giant-size grudge against her?

What was he doing up there?

A drift of smoke wafted to her nose.

No. No.

She whipped around on the stool and went at a dead run for the gaping hole that led to the stage.

Wait. She skidded to a stop, turned and raced back to the bar. Drew had installed a fire extinguisher there before the party. Grappling with the holding hooks, she freed it and ran, praying.

"COME ON, ANSWER, DAMMIT." As restless as a cat, Drew hitched up his jeans. Dressed in his Saturday casual clothes, he balanced a hip on the corner of his desk and scowled down at the telephone. "Where in the hell are you, anyway?" But the phone rang endlessly in his ear.

He slammed the useless instrument into its cradle. If somebody didn't answer in Shadow Gap within the next twenty minutes, he'd bully Court's pilot into taking him to South Dakota and let Court fire them both when he came back.

THE EXTINGUISHER WEIGHED A TON, and Diana's hands were slick with perspiration. She hadn't a prayer of dragging it up those narrow, winding stairs without clanging it against the iron and letting the intruder know she was coming. But she had to try.

She was almost to the top when she smelled the smoke. Potent and strong, it nearly choked her. In her desperate need to hurry, the extinguisher slipped. The resounding clang reverberated through the building with the clarity of a mountain call.

She raced through the connecting doors. There, in a corner of the bedroom, flames smoldered inside a tackle box. She squeezed the handle of the extinguisher, pulled the pin and directed the nozzle at the flames, covering them with white foam.

A few seconds later she leaned against the wall, exhausted, trembling with relief that the fire was out, silence echoing around her.

The intruder. She flew to the window and saw Ron, making his rounds. Better late than never. Maybe if she hurried, she could join forces with him and they could find the creep. If they caught him on the premises, it would be hard for him to deny his wrongdoing.

She ran to the door that led out into the hallway and tugged furiously. It wouldn't budge. She pulled again.

It stayed solidly in place. She rattled the iron knob. The door was locked.

Frantic, she ran to the other door leading into the dressing room. Funny. She couldn't remember closing it. And certainly not this tightly. But it was closed now—and locked. She was trapped. She'd been decoyed up here by a small fire that wasn't going anywhere. He'd known all along exactly where she was and what she would do.

Diana raced to the window. Ron was gone. She knocked on the glass. No answer. Someone besides Ron was out there. The wind hadn't slammed that door shut. Somebody had closed it behind her while she was busy with the fire.

Where was he now? Downstairs, setting a fire that wasn't contained inside a tackle box? Frantic, she whirled around and pounded on the door, kicking and screaming. Only the wind answered. The wind that would take a fire through Shadow Gap and leave nothing but cinders in its wake.

IT WAS ELEVEN by the time the pilot got the flight plan filed and the engine checked and fueled, and it was noon before Drew's plane got clearance for takeoff from Logan. They'd be three hours in the air. Drew laid his head back in the high leather executive chair and tried to tell himself he was going on a wild-goose chase. There couldn't be anything wrong. But a voice inside his head told him there could be no good reason for that site phone to ring unanswered.

DIANA PULLED AT THE HANDLE of the window. It was painted shut, just like the one in the Victorian house.

She strained to hear the sound of crackling fire. Was the smoke smell growing stronger? She didn't think so.

She paced, thinking there must be something she could do. She could break the window. And then what? Risk a fall from twenty-five feet up and break most of the major bones in her body? Not a good idea. She wouldn't do that until she was sure he meant to burn the hotel. Which, with Ron out there, he probably wouldn't.

Diana glanced at her watch. Only thirty-five minutes had gone by since she'd first smelled the smoke and she wasn't smelling anymore. But it seemed as if she'd been trapped for thirty-five hours. Where was Ron?

She couldn't bear to stay in this room for an hour. But it seemed she had little choice. Ron would walk around to check each of the doors at five o'clock, when the shift changed. She should be able to get his attention then. She steeled herself to pace and sit and wait. And pray.

AFTER WHAT SEEMED like the longest hours of his life, Drew drove up to Shadow Gap and was greeted by Ron at the gate. "Where have you been?" Drew snapped.

Ron looked sheepish. "Right here."

"Like hell."

"I was helping a lady in distress." Looking red faced and defensive, Ron recounted the story of the lady with the flat tire and how, when they'd finally found someone to fix it, the lady had insisted on buying his dinner while they were waiting, and they got to talking and she was nice looking and . . .

"You haven't seen Diana?"

Ron shook his head.

"Don't you find that a little odd, since her car's here?" Ron gave him a blank look. Drew grimaced. "Come on; I might need your muscle."

Diana looked out the window, expecting to see nothing. Drew strode into view, looking like a hurricane bearing down on the coast. Her heart thudding with joy, she knocked furiously on the window.

He looked up, and when he saw her, the expression on his face was so strange it was nearly comical. Relief chased away the worry, and exasperation chased away the relief.

He said something to her that might have been "What in hell are you doing up there?" She shook her head and shrugged her shoulders. What did he think she was doing, painting her fingernails? She held a fist up to the window and made a turning motion with her wrist as if unlocking a door. Drew shook his head in disbelief and disappeared somewhere below her.

He came into the hotel running, Ron behind him. "Take the stairs . . ." he yelled. "I'm going up the back way."

At the exact time that Ron fit the key in the lock and unlocked the door, Drew yanked open the wedged door in the side wall.

Diana stared at both men. "Well, you'd think with two sets of cavalry, one of you could have got here a little quicker."

Drew took in the destruction in the room with one swift glance. "What happened here?"

She was trembling with her relief at seeing him. She couldn't let him know how frightened she'd been, or that she knew who'd lured her up here. "I've been playing hide-and-seek. Only the guy I'm playing with cheated. He locked me in so he could hide but I couldn't seek."

Drew wasn't in the mood for a flip answer. He took a step toward her, his face like a thundercloud. Then he stopped and turned to Ron. "Go look around outside and see if you can see anybody. That's what she's paying you for—not to fix flat tires for good-looking women."

Ron turned beet red. "Yes, sir."

Diana cocked an eyebrow at Drew. "How did you know the woman he helped was good-looking?"

"He told me so. But if he hadn't, I'd have guessed." He came closer. "Tell me what happened."

She did. When she'd finished, he'd backed her into a corner and was wearing his hurricane look again. "You smelled a fire and dragged that extinguisher up those iron stairs? You knew somebody was up here and you came up, anyway?"

"I thought he was going to set the place on fire." Her chin rose a notch. "What would you have done, Drew?"

He'd have done exactly the same thing, and they both knew it. "Called the fire department."

"And had half the town burned down by the time they got here? Or had them come roaring out on what might have been a false alarm?"

A muscle moved in his cheek, but Diana knew it wasn't amusement he was suppressing. He looked as if he wanted to strangle her. Instinctively she knew she had to comfort him.

"I'm all right, Drew." Relief swept over her, making her trembly.   Anguish bit deeply into Drew. He'd been abrasive because he'd been so afraid for her, while she tossed her fears aside and thought only of reassuring him. He was so damn new at this, caring for a woman.

He loved her too much to—He loved her. He knew that now. He loved her with the same desperation, the same needy hope that his father loved Ruth. He'd promised himself long ago that he'd never love any woman so obsessively, but now he saw that even though he'd tried to keep his feelings for Diana in a nice, neat box, he hadn't succeeded. She was his life. If anything had happened to her, he wouldn't have wanted to live.

Filled with an emotion too strong to contain, he swept her into his arms and covered her mouth with a possessive kiss, telling her in the only way he could how desperately and completely he loved her.

AN HOUR LATER, Diana stepped out of the shower cubicle in the trailer, wrapped in her towel.

Drew sat at the small dining table reading a South Dakota paper. When he saw her, he put the paper down and thrust his knees into the aisle, making it impossible for her to walk past him.

"Drew, you'll have to move. I have to get by you to get to my clothes. . . ."

He caught the edge of the towel she'd tucked in above her breasts. "Why?"

"I need to get dressed." Diana liked the way he looked in his Saturday jeans and his Saturday smile. He was also wearing that mock-serious look she'd learned to distrust.

"Why, Diana?"

Blue eyes met green. "I thought you were taking me out to dinner."

"I am. But I didn't say when." He pulled her onto his lap and nuzzled her soap-scented neck.

His mouth was hot and sweet against her skin. She tilted her head back, luxuriating in the possessiveness of his caresses. She liked the feel of his arm around her waist, the hard muscles in his thighs supporting her.

"Diana," he murmured, his drawl as smooth as silk, "there's something I need to know."

"What...is it?" Warmth. His lips bathed her in a hot, sweet warmth that made her bones melt and her skin come alive with desire.

"How to turn this table into a bed."

Clutching at her towel and laughing, she showed him.

After a long, sweet time of loving, Diana nestled her head deeper into the hollow of Drew's shoulder. She didn't want to think about what had happened at Shadow Gap. She wanted to lie in Drew's arms and savor the wonderful languor that his lovemaking gave her. Most of all, she didn't want him to come to the same conclusion she had about the identity of the man causing the damage in Shadow Gap. She didn't want him to do anything to confront her nemesis head on. Which was what Drew would do if he had half a chance. Catching the culprit was her job. The only problem was—she hadn't quite figured out how to do it.

"Diana."

He leaned over her, his eyes dark, their depths slumberous with the same languor that pervaded her body. "You do know who's causing the trouble, don't you?"

She turned, hugging him closer. "I know who I *think* is doing it. But there's nothing we can do to prove it."

His mouth firmed, and she knew she'd said the wrong thing. No one told a Lindstrom man there was something he couldn't do. "There's something I can do."

"Whatever gets done, we do it together."

He was silent for a moment as if marshaling his arguments. "Maybe you're right." He pulled the sheet back and bent his head to her breast. "The things we do together we do to perfection."

It was ten o'clock at night by the time they rolled into Shadow Gap. The eerie, empty buildings flashed by, one by one. As Diana got out of the car and stood outside the hotel waiting, Drew drove around to the other side of the Fargo building to hide the car. A night bird cried, sending a chill up Diana's spine. The canyons loomed too close. Even the light breeze through the trees seemed to whisper, *Foolish woman.*

Drew materialized in the dark, and she started.

"I should have left you in the trailer." Drew's arm came around her shoulders. "Diana, this could get dangerous."

"I doubt it. He's too much of a coward."

In the end, as Drew had known he would, he let her climb the stairs with him into the second-floor hallway of the hotel, where they both slid down the wall to the floor. They faced the open door of the purple-papered bedroom. And waited.

With the small penlight they'd bought, Diana dug into her purse and came up with a prize. "Want a peanut?"

He stared at the thin pencil stream of light to see what she held in her hand. "They're in the shell."

"What's wrong with that?"

Drew made an exasperated sound. "Do you think he's going to come up here to claim that tackle box if he hears you cracking peanut shells?"

"My brother-in-law eats them when he's nervous. I thought I'd try it."

Drew grasped her shoulders and pulled her around so that she could see his face in the thin sliver of light. "If there was any real danger, you wouldn't be here. You know that, don't you? Bridges has been very careful to keep his damage on the nuisance level. He's a contractor, a businessman. But I did some investigating this week. His wife is divorcing him and asking for a large sum of money. At the same time, his company is floundering. He wasn't feeling too happy toward women the day he walked into our town. He was looking for trouble."

To Diana, it all sounded very cool and logical, exactly the way Drew would see things. But she wondered if Bridges was as self-contained as Drew believed him to be. "And he's taking his frustrations out on me?"

"Something like that."

"When you called him . . . he didn't deny it was his tackle box?"

Drew frowned. "Yes, he denied it. But he sounded . . . shaken."

"You didn't tell him who you were?"

"I'm not a fool," he drawled. "I disguised my voice and told him I worked security for you and for twenty dollars, I'd see to it the alarm was off if he came and got it tonight. If he didn't come for it right away, I couldn't guarantee anything, because my buddy would be working the night shift next week."

"Have you ever thought you might have a criminal mind?" Diana relaxed, trying to get more comfortable on the hard floor. "Don't you think you're working a little cheap—twenty dollars?"

"I'm a small-time crook."

"He may sense it's a trap and not show up at all."

"He'll show up."

A few minutes later, in the quiet of the premidnight hour, the hotel creaked. Instantly Drew flicked the light off. In the darkness Diana's skin prickled. Drew's hand gripped her arm, warning her silently not to move. But as they sat there frozen, the hotel echoed with silence.

"False alarm," Drew said in a low tone.

Diana laid her head back against the wall, her heart pounding. "When I contracted to renovate this ghost town, I didn't know I was going to be the ghost."

How he loved her sense of humor. How he loved her. It was time he told her so. He raised her hand to his mouth and brushed her fingers with his lips. "I love you. You know that, don't you?"

He was lucky she couldn't see well enough in the dark to hit him. What a time he picked to say the words she'd been aching to hear for so long. "You are the most exasperating man—"

"Shh." His sharp command to be silent brought the hair up on her nape. "I think he's here."

"Suppose he comes up the main stairs instead of the back one?"

"If he does, he'll trip over us. On your feet, woman."

His elbow under her arm, he dragged her upright with him as he came up off the floor. She stood listening to the darkness, the only reality the warmth of Drew's hand gripping hers.

The soft sluff-sluff of shoes on the iron treads of the back stairway reverberated through the old building and sang along her nerves. Drew's hand tightened on her fingers.

The glow from a flashlight siphoned into the bedroom from the open door of the changing room. It grew brighter, gradually lighting up the room until a hulking form stepped into their view and reached for the tackle box.

"Stop right there." Drew's voice cracked through the darkness. The man whipped around and flashed his light in Drew's eyes. Instantly Drew reached for the light switch inside the bedroom and flicked it on.

A frightened, startled, angry Tom Bridges stood facing them. "What in hell—" Comprehension swept over his face. "So it was a setup. I should have known. Did you call the cops?"

"I have a man at the security shack waiting for a word from me to do that . . . if it's necessary."

Bridges stood watching them warily, as if he expected them to rush him. "If you're not going to turn me in, then why did you drag me up here?"

"To show you we're on to you. If my contractor has any more trouble here in Shadow Gap, she and I will have you indicted and prosecuted to the full extent of the law. But if you pick up that tackle box and walk out of here and don't come back, that will be the end of it. It's your choice."

Bridges glared at them. "Hell. I didn't want to hurt anybody. I just wanted to teach Miss Smartypants there a lesson."

A hot retort on her lips, Diana started forward, but Drew grasped her wrist and held her back. "We guessed as much. You could have done real damage here if you hadn't been careful about the fire. But you didn't want me to have any real complaint to file against you, did you?"

"Are you gonna' talk law or are you gonna' let me go?"

"Are you going to stay away from Shadow Gap and leave me and mine alone?"

Bridges snorted. "I wouldn't come near this place again if you paid me."

"Understand this." Drew took a step toward Bridges. "If you're lying and you show up here again, I won't wait for the law to come after you. I'll come after you myself. Is that clear?"

"As crystal."

"Then I suggest you get out of here as fast as you can before I change my mind about calling the police."

"WHY DIDN'T YOU WAKE ME?" Diana yawned and stretched. The light and heat in the trailer told her it was well into the afternoon.

"You'd had a hard night. You needed your sleep." Drew ran a lazy finger down her arm.

She folded the sheet over her breasts and under her arms and stretched her legs, feeling like a cat who'd just had a long, luxurious sleep in the sun. She turned to look at the man who lounged in the bed beside her. "You're quite impressive when you threaten somebody who's forty pounds heavier and two inches taller and has a mean temper."

"A skill I learned from dealing with my father," Drew said.

"Remind me not to get on your bad side. Are you hungry?"

"Not ... quite ... yet." His darkening eyes told her what he was hungry for.

She turned to him and stroked a hand down his face lovingly, smiling at him. "You're a very bad man, do you know that?"

"That isn't what you said when you were making love this morning."

"Now, there, you see. That just proves how bad you are. A gentleman wouldn't remind a lady of what she said when."

"Diana. You don't have to work so hard at keeping things light."

He was too perceptive for his own good. She said, "I'm not working to keep things light—"

"Yes, you are. You're trying to be light and bright and sophisticated." He moved over her, partially resting his chest on her breasts, one elbow propping his head up. "I appreciate your brave effort, sweetheart; I really do." He kissed the rounded flesh above the sheet. "But you're wasting it."

"Wasting it?" Between trying to concentrate on what he was saying and staving off the rising warmth his mouth was spreading, she couldn't think at all.

Drew knew that even though he'd told her he loved her, she'd need to hear it again. And again. He wouldn't mind repeating it at all. He would keep saying it until she believed it. "You do love me, don't you?" He touched her mouth gently with the tip of his finger.

Her breath came out in a long sigh. "You know I do."

His smile was beautiful to behold—Drew in all his glory. That same finger traced down her throat to the top of the sheet. "I love you, Diana," he said with such elegant simplicity, it took her breath away. "And if you'll have me, I'm here to stay, in whatever way we can work it out until you finish the outer construction in Shadow Gap at the end of next month. I'll fly here on weekends, or you can fly to Boston. After that, we can be married." He flattened his palm on the bed beside her, looming over her—tanned, glorious, wonderful man. Her man. "Do you believe me?"

How could she not? His eyes were bright with possessiveness, his mobile mouth lifted in the tantalizing start of a smile that would always send a chill up her spine. "I believe you, Drew."

He set about proving it with his hands and his mouth, and when he murmured those wonderful words to her, telling her how beautiful she was and how much he wanted her, she knew beyond a shadow of a doubt that she was the one love of his heart, just as he was hers.

Epilogue

A POWDERY, DELICATE SNOW feathered through the sky over Shadow Gap. Christmas lights twinkled like diamonds on the peaked roof of the Oliver house and winked from the roof of the hotel. Typically cantankerous to the end, the Fargo building kept blowing a fuse on its string of lights. Drew had managed to thwart the old building by running a line from the bank to keep the lights lit for the evening of December 20.

The cold weather only served to add to the high spirits of the crowd in the old hotel. Court was giving another of his famous parties. Jeanine, flashing a bright smile and a diamond ring to match, was passing the hors d'oeuvres. This party was for the friends and family of all Diana's crew, as well as for several of the men in the Bernice Foods organization. The saloon was decorated in Christmas finery, festooned with looped garlands of green over the bar and staircase. Bright red candles glowed at each end of the bar and at the tables set up in front of the stage. A Christmas tree with winking lights decorated the right side of the stage. Strung from one side of the new, red-velvet stage curtain to the other was a wide red satin ribbon waiting to be cut by the newly appointed mayor of Shadow Gap, a young woman whose name had been drawn by lottery from those people present.

Thad lifted a punch cup to his lips. "So this is what you two have been doing all year?"

Ruth, standing next to him, said a soft, chiding word.

"Well, not exactly all, father." Drew smiled a slow, secretive smile at Diana and lifted her hand to his mouth, the gold band on his third finger gleaming in the bright light. In his black tux with red cummerbund, a red rose in his lapel, he was heart-melt material. And she wasn't the only one who thought so. Several of the women there tonight had given him a discreet once-over. Luckily for them, Drew hadn't spared them a glance. His eyes sought out Diana's constantly, just as hers seemed unable to look anywhere but at him. She'd worn her red dress tonight in honor of the occasion— the one with an extra inch in the waist.

Thad grunted. "A town. What kind of a contribution is that? Now, Blake here, he's got something to be proud of. He's got a son."

Drew's eyes lifted to Diana's. *Some things never change*, his said.

Hers answered with a gleam, *They will. They will.*

Standing beside Drew, Blake's smile echoed his cousin's.

"Where are Jamie and the baby?" Diana asked.

"She went to feed him. Jordan likes his meals regularly. He doesn't understand about Christmas parties."

"So speaks the proud papa," Diana teased.

Blake slanted a look at Drew. "I hear you're joining the ranks of proud fathers."

Thad spilled his punch. "What? What?"

Ruth produced a handkerchief and began wiping the front of Thad's suit. "It's a good thing you wore your dark blue suit instead of the gray."

Drew lifted a mocking eyebrow and looked at his wife. "You told Jamie?"

Diana shook her head. "I told Jenny and she told her mother and her mother told Blake. She has such a sweet, innocent face, that Jenny. She makes you believe she can keep a secret. She's going to be dangerous, that girl." She put her hand on Thad's arm. "I'd speak to Drew about this, Thad. After all, he promised you you'd be the first to know."

"Don't incite him to riot, sweetheart," Drew said. "My father doesn't need encouragement like that." His smile was affectionate, indulgent. He enjoyed seeing his wife and his father together.

"Tarnation! Are you going to have a baby or aren't you?"

"Are," said Diana, her smile bright.

"Well. Well. Maybe you did do something this year that's worthwhile after all, son."

"An accolade from my father. This moment calls for a celebration." Drew lifted his punch glass and flashed a smile over it at Diana that was beautiful to behold. If she was lucky, her baby would have that same smile, the smile she would wait for, and love, the rest of her life.

Temptation™

TEMPTATION WILL BE EVEN HARDER TO RESIST...

In September, Temptation is presenting a sophisticated new face to the world. A fresh look that truly brings Harlequin's most intimate romances into focus.

What's more, all-time favorite authors Barbara Delinsky, Rita Clay Estrada, Jayne Ann Krentz and Vicki Lewis Thompson will join forces to help us celebrate. The result? A very special quartet of Temptations...

- **Four striking covers**
- **Four stellar authors**
- **Four sensual love stories**
- **Four variations on one spellbinding theme**

All in one great month! Give in to Temptation in September.

HARLEQUIN SIGNATURE EDITION

VIOLET WINSPEAR

HOUSE OF STORMS

Editorial secretary Debra Hartway travels to the Salvador family's rugged Cornish island home to work on Jack Salvador's latest book. Disturbing questions hang in the troubled air over Lovelis Island. What or who had caused the tragic death of Jack's young wife? Why did Jack stay away from the home and, more especially, the baby son he loved so well? And—why should Rodare, Jack's brother, who had proved himself a man of the highest integrity, constantly invade Debra's thoughts with such passionate, dark desires...?

Violet Winspear, who has written more than 65 romance novels translated worldwide into 18 languages, is one of Harlequin's best-loved and bestselling authors. HOUSE OF STORMS, her second title in the Harlequin Signature Edition program, is a full-length novel rich in romantic tradition and intriguingly spiced with an atmosphere of danger and mystery.

Watch for HOUSE OF STORMS—coming in October! HOFS-1